KATHARINE WANG

THE **KING** OF
SALEM
*and the blueprints for
the new heaven and new earth*

AGE TO COME
UNIVERSITY PRESS

ATCU Press
Ashburn, VA

Find the authors online at ATCUniversity.com.

Cover design by Amy Youssef, WaterKress Creative
www.waterkress.com

ONLINE MATERIAL AVAILABLE

Listen to Don and Katharine guide you through
the book in the corresponding online material.

Learn more at Age to Come University
www.ATCUniversity.com

Contents

TO THE KING OF SALEM

May you touch the lives of the people who read about you
here as deeply as you've touched our lives

Acknowledgments

This is the first book we've written together and the first book either of us has authored with someone else. To say that we were doubly blessed by working as a team would be an understatement. When two people walk together, their power doesn't get added together. It's not multiplied together. The expansion is exponential. And in this case, that's true across multiple dimensions. Combining two earthly and heavenly teams unleashed power, insight, and, we believe, the ability to transform lives–exponentially.

On earth, we'd like to thank Gina Green for meticulously proofreading the manuscript. Her careful attention to detail and relentless quest to create an amazing fantasy story is evident in every chapter. Many thanks to Amy Youssef, founder of WaterKress Creative (www.waterkress.com), for her cover design of both the paper and audiobook versions of the book. Amy's ability to see beauty and majesty has helped us all step more fully into the world of Salem.

Special thanks to Don's friend Marios Ellinas for his insights into the city of Salem, especially the point that Salem was the city Hebrews 11 references as the place Abraham was searching for. We'd also like to acknowledge Ian Clayton for introducing the three kings, including the King of Salem, to the world in the way he did. His teaching made this book possible.

Many thanks to our heavenly teams, too. Time doesn't permit us to tell you all the ways the angels and beings who attend us worked to take this project from a few visions we thought we may as well write down to a book that is launching with a worldwide audience.

Lastly, and perhaps most importantly, we'd like to thank our Insiders. Very few first-time co-authors launch a series with so many people from all over the globe cheering it on from its inception. We truly value our

Insiders. We feel blessed to share our lives with you. We look forward to walking together and getting to know many of you much more deeply over time.

Above everything else, we thank Yahweh. To him and through him and for him everything exists. That includes this book. It includes the series this book launches. And it includes our lives. Praise and glory be to him, and to his kingdom, both now and forever!

Preface

If I could choose to enter earth's timeline whenever I wanted, it would be now. Everything is about to change. What's enslaved us for eons will disappear so drastically that those things will be hard to recall. Death, disease, lack, and brokenness will be found only in history books. Only the most astute archeologists will be familiar with them. The blueprint for how this radical transformation will happen is being released now. A new heaven and a new earth will emerge.

We get to be the people who build it.

Sure, if you entered earth a century or two from now, things may be easier. Embracing life, abundance, and wholeness wouldn't require flowing against the current. But then you'd be following the gateways others opened. Those alive right now are the ones who get to establish a new era for humanity. Like the founders of a new nation, we're the ones who explore uncharted territory that will later bear our names. We're the ones who write and speak about our ideas—ideas that get recorded in the documents that shape not just a nation but the entire universe. Every gateway we open, we'll enter. But we won't enter as people following a path others forged. We'll be the ones who's spiritual DNA, whose very essences, are those gateways into what all of heaven and earth—every single dimension of existence—has been yearning for since the beginning.

This book is about being part of that process.

HOW WE WROTE THIS BOOK

Don spoke at a three-day conference in Hastings, New Zealand. The theme of the event was "The Blueprints of the New Heaven and Earth."

A few weeks before the conference, the spiritual being, the King of Salem, asked me to spend three days at his house in the heavenly realms and record the encounters in a book. Around that time, Don began preparing for the conference. At one point, he told me he felt he was half living at the conference, peering into what heaven wanted to release. "I feel like I'm half living in the King of Salem's house," I replied. "And I have a feeling it's linked to the conference."

The day after I mentioned to Don that I was hanging out at the King of Salem's house, Don entered the adventure, becoming a main character. From that moment on, his presence overshadowed the encounters, releasing a higher level of revelation and insight. The book transformed from a private, three-day visit to a royal, inter-galactic event celebrating the release of the blueprints for the new heaven and new earth.

As it turns out, many of the all-star lineup that connected with me at the King of Salem's house in the weeks before the conference were also meeting with Don, preparing him for what needed to happen at that event. Don's talk at the conference is included as part of the story here. Many things released spiritually at that conference are woven into our adventure.

But this story isn't about that conference. It's much broader than a single event. It's about how to unlock the highest purposes for your life—so you can do what you came here to do in a way that exceeds your wildest dreams. And, by the way, that will include building what heaven and earth have been longing for, too.

HOW TO READ THE BOOK

This isn't a theology book. It's a story. It's an adventure. But it's not your typical fantasy adventure story. Every word is a portal. Every scene is an invitation.

The spiritual beings who appear in the book came because they want to interact with each person who reads the book. For many, you found this book because they called to you. What's written in your heart, in the scroll of your life, resonates with who they are. And it's time to connect.

Or it's time to go deeper into the connection you already have.

Similarly, every place mentioned, every artifact discovered, and every detail in the book is a doorway into what was written about. You can step into any of it. Go as deep as you dare. It's all there to bless you and draw out your highest potential.

So take the story in whatever way benefits you the most. Read it as an adventure. Read it as a parable. Consider it an invitation.

Except for the chapters recording Don's talk at the conference, the story unfolded for me as a series of encounters. I experienced the events and then wrote them down. Sometimes, I could interact with the vision, influencing how things unfolded. Sometimes, it refused input from my mind. I simply watched. Occasionally, I'd pass along a chapter or two to Don. Sometimes, he knew what our spirit beings were doing without my telling him. After completing the entire adventure, we worked together to shape it into its current form.

Because this is far more than a story, you may wish to read the book multiple times. Ask Understanding to walk with you through every page. Step into the scenes yourself. If you're reading this book, then you were there. You were at the party and conference the King of Salem hosted at his house. You dined in his banqueting halls. You danced in his ballrooms. You journeyed into his city. As you read, find yourself. Where were you at the party? Which table did you sit at for dinner? Who did you talk to? Where did you stay? Who did you dance with or share a glass of wine with? This isn't a story you're reading. It's a living adventure you were part of and can enter into again and again.

As you turn the page and step into the events recorded here, may life never be the same for you. May you, from this moment forward, become all that the deepest places in your heart have longed to be. And may you never look back. Because the best days of your life don't lie in that direction. The best days of your life are entangled with your highest potentials. And your highest potentials are entangled with the greatest day the earth will ever know. As you pierce one, the other will burst open in response.

It's time to burst some things open.

Katharine Wang & Don Joseph

Day 1

Chapter 1

I was expecting something over the top. He was one of the wealthiest kings in the realms, after all. He probably didn't know how to do ordinary levels of riches and grandeur. So, from the moment he invited me, I had begun to mentally brace myself for what spending three days at his house may be like.

Now, I stood in his formal library, countless books soaring for two stories above my head. Mesmerized, I watched him drop giant ice cubes into a glass. As he poured a strong, caramel-colored liquor over the ice, I glanced at his face.

I had accepted his invitation to spend time with him at his estate because I considered it an honor to be invited. Every other time I had seen him, he had intimidated me. But now his features seemed more relaxed, less threatening.

"I like you, Katharine," he began as extended the drink he had just poured. "That's why I invited you here so soon. I don't normally invite people inside these doors so quickly after I meet them."

"There's something about you that I'm drawn to," I confessed. "It's not your riches or your power or your knowledge. Something underneath all that—the thing that drives everything you do—that's what intrigues me."

"Well said," he smiled. "I want you to meet some of my friends."

When I turned around, I was surprised to discover two men sitting on the library's opulent furniture. I immediately recognized them.

THE THREE KINGS

Until a few months ago, when someone mentioned "the three kings," I thought they were referring to the wise men in children's Christmas stories. Then, I heard Ian Clayton teaching about three heavenly kings who would play a major role in building the new heaven and new earth the Bible talked about. After Ian introduced these kings to the world, other people began interacting with them, too.

My host, the King of Salem, was one of these kings. The King of Righteousness and the King of Peace were the others. Those two kings sat in the library, dressed as regally as my host. Like the King of Salem, they cut to the chase.

"We want to extend to you a formal offer to work with us," the King of Righteousness announced.

He gestured for me to sit with them on the sofas.

"You've had enough time to think about it. There are things we'd like to start working on immediately."

He presented a formal legal document to me. I always took these kinds of offers seriously. I knew they could shift things powerfully in the natural world as well as the spiritual.

"Read all the provisions," the king advised. "Be sure you know what you're getting yourself into."

These three kings were tasked with administering the Mountain—or the spiritual space—where the blueprints of the new heaven and new earth were housed. From there, they would facilitate people on earth accessing the blueprints, understanding their role, and receiving what they need to build.

They weren't asking me to simply take the part of the blueprint I was to administer. They were asking me to work with them in a broader way. I wanted to know what their ultimate objective was.

"Our goal is to restore the glory of the earth," the King of Righteousness explained. "We're recruiting people who share our vision—leaders in various areas—to work with us."

Who wouldn't want to be part of that? I thought. Aloud, I asked, "What's the downside of saying yes?"

"Opportunity cost," he answered.

"Things I won't be able to pursue as fully because I'm doing this?" I clarified.

"And there are some other things. Read up," he directed, sliding the contract across the coffee table.

THE CONTRACT

A half smile crossed my face as I read through the contract. One provision required me to do "extended travel for work," meaning visions that would take me to distant places for long periods of time. In another provision, I'd agree that my body be a full participant in the contract—allowing technologies and upgrades to be fully integrated and activated in my physical body. I'd have to agree to liaison with important angels and representatives from other species of beings. I'd have an office—a spiritual space to study and do this work. I'd be given a staff, some of which would come from the internal staff of the three kings who sat around the small table with me.

"I'm going to say yes," I announced. "But not because of your fancy contract or your wealth or your position. I'm drawn to who you are. There's something about you I like. I want to be near it. I want to let you into my life."

"You won't regret it," the King of Salem smiled.

"I don't intend to," I grinned back at him. "Now, if you'll hand me a pen, we can make it official."

So, I signed my name to their contract. And then it sunk in that I had just agreed to do extensive spiritual work with three kings I barely knew. In one gulp, I downed my drink to calm my nerves.

"Training starts immediately," the King of Righteousness announced, folding the signed contract and slipping it into his robe. "You're the head of recruitment."

That's when I realized I hadn't asked what I'd be doing.

"We want you to know this place—this house and the city that goes with it—extremely well."

"Know all the details," the King of Peace spoke for the first time.

"Write it down, at least in your mind, if you can't put it on paper," the King of Salem directed. "I'll give you a personal tour soon. There's a lot to do. But I don't want our connection to be all work. Spend a few more days with me here as my guest. Let's get to know each other better. Then I'll open my personal storehouses and show you around officially. Write everything down. Document it. You'll need to know all this for what you do."

"We like your keen eye," the King of Peace interjected. "Watch for details. You'll be telling scores of people about us one day. You'll share some of what we show you to your grandkids—the adventures you had with us."

"There's a lot to do," the King of Righteousness stood. "We'll leave you to your day. Come speak with us later."

Chapter 2

As the kings stood, two servants entered to escort me to the guest chambers. The King of Salem shooed them away.

"I'll show Katharine to her quarters," he told them good-naturedly. Extending his elbow to me, he motioned for us to go.

Walking side by side, he led us through the maze of hallways to the guest rooms on the upper level. I used this opportunity to study him in more detail. I realized he was a spirit, taking on a human form to make it easier for me to relate to him. I also realized that different people may perceive him differently. We filter the information we perceive in the spiritual realm through our cultural and personal lenses. So, spirits like him may look different ways to different people. We're all perceiving the same information flow. But we're filtering it through our lenses to create the image that best fits the information for us.

To me, the King of Salem looked young and handsome. His light brown hair fell in large locks around his flawless face. When he smiled, the room lit up—ready to center itself around his command. His clothes were regal, spun from thick threads. He wore them in several layers so they perfectly accentuated his masterful presence.

But what intrigued me about him wasn't his costly garments or stunning features. I had met countless people and angels in heaven who were equally captivating. What drew me to him was a particular flow in his essence. Streaming from him was every attribute, every thought, every part of who he is. When certain aspects of him hit me, I wanted more. I couldn't put my finger on exactly what intrigued me about the King of Salem. But if I had to put it in words, I'd call it grandeur mixed with worth, intelligence, and boldness to get the job done. He was intimidatingly no-nonsense. But he had a tender, personal side that let people in deeply.

That part of him opened to me as he escorted me to my quarters. Although we walked in silence, inwardly, without words, he made it clear that he wanted us to know each other well. The contract I had just signed guaranteed that we'd be working together. Now, it seemed he wanted a more personal connection, too. Could I ever consider this formidable king a friend? I wondered. Glancing at his imposing figure as we rounded a corner, I wasn't sure.

"Here we are," he stopped in front of an oversized door with hand-carved trim along its borders.

"Would you like to come in? I can pour you a drink," I offered.

"Some other time," he smiled. "My staff will come to brief you on some things. Then I'll be back later myself."

Hearing his promise to come himself, I stiffened involuntarily. His presence was so intimidating that I wondered if I could ever fully relax around him.

"We have a lot we could do together," he smiled. "Enjoy your afternoon."

Chapter 3

For several minutes, I explored my room. A queen bed lay in the far corner. At the foot of the bed, a window overlooked the back of the mansion. Sunlight was streaming through the sheer curtains, giving a bright glow to the room.

Against the right-hand wall, a gorgeous desk stood. Its white wood was etched with elegant hand carvings. A light pink writing pad covered the entire center of the desk, giving it a feminine flare. Running my hand down its carvings, I smiled. The King of Salem had given me this room so I could write—with heaven's pen—as I stayed here.

Hesitantly, I opened the door to the walk-in closet. Elegant clothes for all occasions hung neatly on the left side of the closet. Matching shoes lined cubby holes on the right side. He had certainly made sure I could be dressed for any activity during my brief stay.

Shutting the closet door, I migrated towards the desk. A couple of books from the library rested on one corner. Was I meant to read these volumes? I wondered.

I had just picked one up when there was a knock at the door.

"Come in," I called.

I didn't recognize the man who stepped into my room. "I'm here to give you a tour of the house," he announced.

"I thought Salem was going to give me a tour," I replied. I had started calling the King of Salem by his city's name for short.

"He'll give you his own private tour. I'm giving you the public one," the servant answered matter-of-factly. "Come with me, please."

Slipping my shoes back on, I hurried to the door.

"You're not going to lock your door?" the servant asked. "Most people do. It stands for keeping your projects non-public until you're ready to go public with them."

"I don't think anything I'm working on here is secret," I winked. But I locked the door anyway.

"You never know," the servant shrugged. "There's a lot of security around here. You may notice security cameras in various places."

"Have there been break-ins? Things stolen?" I asked, surprised.

"Nothing stolen," he shrugged. "It's standard procedure, I suppose, when you're working on things at the level the king is."

"Of course," I nodded.

On earth, I lived in the Washington, D.C. area in the United States. Half the city has top-secret clearance and can't talk about what they do at work. I was used to not prying and following protocol. Slipping my key into my pocket, I hurried down the hall to keep up with my escort.

THE TOUR

We passed through the hallways in silence. Numerous pictures framed in gold lined the walls. Like my bedroom furniture, the walls and ceilings were etched with elegant hand-carvings. That extravagant detail revealed Salem's wealth. But I wondered if the carvings contained mysteries, too. Were hidden messages carved throughout the house— secrets waiting to be unlocked?

If there were, it wasn't part of the public tour. The servant didn't even reveal the names of the people in the portraits we passed. And he was walking so briskly that I didn't have time to check for name plates in front of the portraits.

"Excuse me, but could you tell me who the people in these portraits are?" I asked. "It seems important."

"The king honors the people and beings who had the greatest influence on his life by hanging a portrait of them in his house," the guide explained. "This hallway honors the people who helped build the kingship part of who he is. Other hallways honor those who influenced other aspects of who he became."

"So I can read the nameplate beside them and—"

"Yes, it's like an interactive tour in and of itself," the guide interrupted. "The king has stored information about who each person is and how they influenced him. You can access that information by touching the nameplate. It's quite educational. But we don't have time now, your majesty. You're welcome to return later and spend as much time as you wish."

"Of course, thank you," I replied, making a mental note to investigate later. Everything was here for a reason. Even the smallest detail could provide a life-changing insight, from the portraits to the engravings on the woodwork.

"Your tour begins in the library," the servant announced, opening double doors to the one room I had already visited.

The colossal space still impressed me. Colorful books lined the off-white shelves for two stories. Elegant furniture rested on thick carpets spread throughout the place. Soft lighting made the study seem almost enjoyable here.

A quick glance revealed eight or ten people scattered around the library, absorbed in books. I hadn't noticed them before.

"Is the king's library open to the public now?" I asked. "Why are so many people here?"

"The king is permitting certain individuals to enter his library to study his collection," the servant answered. "And your writing has opened this space to others, too."

"By describing it, I open a way to access it?" I asked.

"It creates a channel for some. It transports others here instantly," he replied. "If you'll come this way, I can show you—"

"I'll take over from here, thank you," the King of Salem interrupted.

THREE-IN-ONE

I hadn't heard him approach. His presence was both commanding and bright. It filled the atmosphere with excited, joyful hope. I was glad to see him.

"Welcome to my library, Katharine," the king beamed. "I have some volumes here you may have seen before. But many others are rare. They are hard to find elsewhere. I think you'd be fascinated. Tell people that I hereby open my library for proper study. I give permission to those who seek to enrich their knowledge for a purpose that they share with me to come here and learn."

I smiled. He sounded both regal and friendly.

"Let me show you around," he offered, strolling down the rows of books. "You can ask me questions like you're interviewing me. I want people to get to know me."

"May I start with a rather basic question? Who are you?" I inquired.

"I'm mentioned in the Bible," the king answered.

"Sort of. Hebrews 7:1–2 says *Melchizedek* was the king of Salem," I pointed out. "I know you're not Melchizedek. I can interact with you and with him separately. I've heard that you, the King of Righteousness, and the King of Peace are like three in one—like a trinity. Ian Clayton says when you appear to people together, it's in your governmental role. When you appear separately, it's in an individual role. How would you explain it?"

"Look at this glass filled with water," the king pointed to the desk beside us. "When I move the glass, what do you see?"

As he slid the glass across the table, I saw three images of it. The second image flowed from the first. And the third image flowed from the second. It looked like special effects in a movie—making me think there were three glasses. But really, it was one.

"I understand the concept of trinity," I told him. "I've heard it explained in a lot of ways. I get it. But I think you're telling me something more. The water in the glass. That's your relationship to Melchizedek, isn't it?"

The king grinned.

"He's the container. You're the water within it, right?" I pressed. "The three kings—Salem, Righteousness, and Peace—you're a trinitarian expression of the role or function of Melchizedek. You're not him. But you flow from who he is. You help fulfill part of Melchizedek's function. That's why we can see you in the Bible verses about him."

"I like how you put it, Katharine," Salem grinned.

"I've heard that you're—"

"I don't want you to tell people what someone else says about me," Salem announced.

Holding my gaze, Salem placed my hand over his heart.

"Read me yourself. Then tell the world who I am," he directed.

"But I'm going to read what's flowing from you through the channels I have open inside me," I protested. "I have channels open that most people don't. I tend to touch the more personal side of someone."

"I know. That's one reason we chose you," Salem smiled at me. "What do you see inside me, Katharine?"

Looking him in the eye, I breathed deeply, opening to him. "You're smart. There's a lot of intelligence flowing from you. Shrewd. I think you'd be good at business transactions."

Salem chuckled. "What else?"

"I have a feeling that when you want something, you get it. You're approaching me with the confidence of someone who's not used to being told 'no.'"

He laughed loudly. I knew I had hit the nail on the head.

"You want to show me your glory and magnificence," I smiled. "I can feel it on the edges of our interaction. But the channel we're in now is overpowering everything else. You're opening up parts of your depths to me, and it's a bit overwhelming. But in a delightful way."

"Same," he smiled.

"You think I'm overwhelming?" I laughed.

"I think you're many things, Katharine. Surprising more than anything else," he answered. "I have heard about you. And now I get to see you with my own eyes."

I tried to pull my hand from his chest, but he held it there forcefully. "What else do you see about me?" he asked.

His eyes pierced me. "You've been waiting a long time to do what you're about to do with humanity and the universe," I answered. "You intend for everything to run smoothly. This endeavor is extremely important to you. It feels like it's so important that you may deal harshly with those who mess it up on purpose. I may be getting that wrong. I don't want to make you seem harsh. You're important and harsh. But you're also supportive and loving to those you open yourself to."

"That's not entirely off. I may be described as harsh at times," he answered. "But for those who work with me and fulfill their obligations—I will take care of you above and beyond the normal compensation. I make people's wildest dreams come true, Katharine. That's because I can see what people's deep desires are. When they open themselves to me to work with me, I can peer deep inside them. So when I look for compensation to give someone for a job well done, I often give people the desires of their hearts."

"I like that," I smiled involuntarily. Hadn't I just signed a contract to work with him? Did that mean I could get paid with the desires of my heart being fulfilled? Sounded like Yahweh.

Releasing my hand from his grip, he said, "You're invited to dinner tonight. Dress accordingly. I'll see you then."

"What about the rest of my tour?" I asked.

"There'll be plenty of time for that later," Salem replied, walking briskly towards the library door.

Chapter 4

I had the rest of the afternoon to myself. I didn't want to waste a minute. Remembering how Salem told me I'd be interested in his book collection, I searched the shelves.

"May I help you?" a friendly voice asked. "Let me introduce myself. I'm the librarian over the King of Salem's personal library. He's asked me to make myself available to anyone who wants to pick a book or two to read from his collection. If they don't know what to choose, they can ask me. I'll make the perfect selection for them."

What an ingenious idea, I smiled to myself. I loved how heaven was like one grand adventure story.

"Would you like me to pick a book for you?" the librarian pressed.

"Yes, of course," I replied.

A moment later, he returned with a volume entitled *How to Read Ancient Engravings*.

"Perfect," I thanked him. "I had just been thinking about deciphering the engravings I've noticed here."

Holding the book tightly, I thought I'd find a peaceful spot to dig into it. The library was too crowded for my taste. So I wandered down the hall, searching for a suitable space. Rushing down the hallway in the opposite direction was an imposing figure. He wore thick, regal clothes like Salem and the other kings. His long robes looked like they were floating an inch or two above the ground around him as he walked. That's how quickly he was darting to his destination.

COMMITTEE MEETING

But when he saw me, he stopped. "Katharine, come with me," Melchizedek commanded. "I'm heading to a committee meeting. I want you to see this for the book. But keep your mouth shut," he looked at me sternly. "You are not on this committee—not yet. Just listen."

So I followed him down the hall to a door on the left. The dozen or so committee members were already seated around the oval table. Melchizedek walked briskly to his place at the head of the table. His robes swooshed around him with every step, emphasizing his grandeur.

Staff from the committee members' houses sat in chairs lining the walls. I found a seat among them. When Melchizedek took his place, every conversation was hushed. The entire room gave him their attention.

"This is the Distribution Committee," Melchizedek began. "We determine when, what, and to whom things relating to the blueprints of the new heaven and new earth are distributed."

I knew the overall agenda. I was waiting for someone to speak. But I guess that's not how these things work. Bodies were sitting around the table. But the bodies felt like a portal to the house or kingdom of the person whose body was visible. The houses had been founded in different periods of earth's history. I could peer into that kingdom if I focused on one of them. Its wisdom, riches, and essence were available to those around the table.

Each king and queen was enormously powerful. They carried great wealth, tremendous influence, and huge armies that could be sent on any mission. I didn't realize kingdoms as great as these existed.

There was a lot to discuss. What did people need to build the new heaven and new earth? What order did they need to receive it in? How should we determine the best people to distribute things to? What would be the most effective means to distribute things?

The rulers shared a lot of compelling ideas. They backed up their proposals with their own resources and with staff who would accomplish their objectives. I was impressed.

MY REPORT

I had ideas, too. I began to burn with the desire to share my ideas. But Melchizedek's stern warning rang through my head. I kept my mouth shut.

But then one of the queens spoke. "I think Katharine should present her report to the committee."

She bid me to stand at the table. I looked at Melchizedek. When he nodded, I approached the other rulers. Once at the table, I saw that an interactive map of the earth was carved into its surface. Interfacing with it, I could feel what each region on earth felt about the blueprint for the new heaven and new earth. There was also a being, who may have been the consciousness of the map, hovering in the center of the table. She was see-through. I couldn't perceive her from where I sat ten feet from the table. But standing at the table, she could be seen and heard. She could answer questions that any committee member posed.

I had never presented a report in precisely this setting before. I didn't know what to do. As it turns out, I opened myself to them. I could feel each ruler exploring my house, my insides. They took what they needed from my library. They drank what they wanted from my streams. When they were satisfied, they withdrew. I hadn't said a word. But my thoughts were shared far more completely than words could have captured.

As I was about to return to my seat, the queen who asked me to share my report spoke again. "I think Katharine ought to give from her supply to fund her ideas."

Again, I looked at Melchizedek. Again, he nodded. So I lay some of my gold and treasure on the table. I promised some of my staff to help with my ideas. Each of the rulers around the table had already given from their kingdom's storehouses to fund the efforts of the distribution committee.

"I consider it an honor to contribute to your worthy tasks," I announced as I placed my treasures on the table.

What were my ideas? As best as my conscious mind can explain them, I thought the teaching around the Mountain and its blueprints should be consolidated into one place. In words, my thoughts could be expressed as: "Take what is in each of your individual libraries that would be useful for people as they begin to build the blueprints for the new heaven and new earth. Take what is useful from other libraries around the realms. Put it all in one place. Place it in the Mountain itself. Or build a library next to the Mountain. Make everything easier for people to access.

"And consolidate the teaching so people don't have to read fifteen volumes from fifteen perspectives before they know what to do," my thoughts continued. "Take from each of your streams. Make a 'master stream.' Have one message flow. It will make things easier to digest for people just starting. Make the on-ramp as short as possible.

"Then commission translations of some texts into easier-to-understand versions," I finished my thoughts. "Right now, many texts require a high level of maturity to comprehend. If you translate them—dumb them down—many more people can begin working on their part of the task."

"But you'll get stupid things built if the immature build them," a king objected.

"I agree. Start by translating the entry-level concepts. Then translate other texts down a grade level or two—not all the way to kindergarten," I smiled. "You could commission the translation of a few texts as a trial run."

Ultimately, most committee members wanted to try out some of my ideas. That's why I was asked to help fund the project. I felt really drawn to this committee's job. I love making ideas accessible to people in their everyday life.

Chapter 5

When the meeting was dismissed, some of the rulers approached me. They wanted to meet privately. Some wanted to discuss the topic in more depth. Others wanted to get to know me better. After arranging those meetings, I was about to leave when Melchizedek called me.

"What did you think of my little committee?" he asked, grinning. He seemed more relaxed now that the meeting was over. I could tell he thought it was enormously successful.

"You're excited that this piece of it is beginning," I told him. I wasn't answering his words. I was responding to what was flowing from him on a different level.

"Immensely so. Walk with me, Katharine," he urged, stepping into the hall. "People will start flooding in. Some here, in Salem's place. Many more will come to the Mountain itself. I want you to be at the forefront of it. Do you have the keys to the Mountain? And the keys to my storerooms?"

"To the Mountain, yes," I nodded. "I'm pretty sure you gave me a set of keys, but I can't remember for sure."

"No worries," he chuckled. "If I haven't, I will. My storehouses will be sorted through soon. The committee will want everything organized so we can distribute what's needed most urgently to the people able to do the most with it. You understand?"

"Yes, sir," I answered.

"That's all for now, Katharine. Stay super excited—like I am," he urged as he took his leave.

PATIO

Alone again, I wandered the halls. I was determined to delve into Salem's book about ancient carvings. My meanderings lead me to an outdoor patio area. It was a beautiful day. I decided to read outside.

On the patio, though, a considerable number of people were milling around. A bartender waited behind a stand, pouring drinks at people's request. Small, black metal tables were set up at intervals. Was some event going on?

I chose an empty table and was about to plunge into my book when I heard my name called.

"Mind if we join you?" a friend from earth approached. Two heavenly companions flanked him on either side.

"Sure, go ahead," I smiled.

"Katharine, you remember Holiness and Righteousness," Don gestured towards them as he slid his chair out to take a seat. The sound of metal scraping stone pierced the atmosphere briefly. As Don sat at the table next to me—with Holiness and Righteousness sitting across from us— the frequency of his chair sliding into place was released and something shifted in the book. At the time, all I could feel was weight, wisdom, and glory, overshadowing the encounters in a way they hadn't before. Later, I realized that was the moment the plot shifted, too. The book began as an invitation to spend a few private days at Salem's place. When Don entered, it became a regal, three-day celebration of the opening of the Mountain that housed the blueprints for a new heaven and earth.

"Are you here to permanently upgrade the book, or are you making a cameo appearance?" I grinned.

Don smiled in response. "Your project sounded interesting and important. I thought maybe you'd like some help."

"Help is always appreciated," I replied. "Especially from a house like yours. I'm intrigued that you brought these two companions."

Turning to Holiness and Righteousness, I said, "What an honor to see you here. May I ask why you're accompanying Don?"

"I have a message for the book," Holiness spoke first, sliding a written note across the table. "Don't read it before Chapter 3."

"I think we're past Chapter 3," I grinned.

"Read it now, then," he urged.

HOLINESS

As I unfolded his note, a wave of his essence hit me. Holiness himself had written the words on the page. They carried his weight and glory. Although I was reading his note, I heard his voice in my head like he was speaking each word to me. The words resonated on many levels and frequencies. I realized he was releasing a message that would hit people in different ways, with varying levels of intensity.

"I've always loved humanity. But my love for and interest in humanity has never been greater than it is in this moment. I am going to be part of opening a new era for humanity. You will be able to access your own holiness in much deeper ways than ever before. You will walk in mature holiness. You will see me in my true, full, mature nature. You will possess me fully. And for those who find me early and embrace me soon, I will reveal myself like I never have before."

When I finished reading the note, I looked across the table at Holiness. I was whirling from the weight of his words.

"There's more, but that's all I have the strength to convey to humanity right now," he said.

"Thank you," I smiled.

I turned to Righteousness. With a broad smile, he said, "My message for the book comes later. Right now, people are just supposed to meet me."

"I see," I nodded. I looked at Don to see if he had anything to add.

"I'm excited," he announced.

"Yes, I can feel some of your excitement," I laughed.

"It's really starting, Katharine," he leaned in to emphasize his point. "Salem is opening this up officially."

"This is some sort of welcoming event, isn't it? The bartender, these tables—we're at a cocktail party on the library patio, aren't we?" I remarked. "There are a ton of people here."

"This is just the beginning of the festivities," Don explained.

"Is that why you three are so dressed up?" I asked, glancing at their tuxedos. "It's a bit much for an afternoon cocktail party—unless Salem is that fancy."

"There's a formal event tonight," Don winked. "Are you coming?"

"Salem invited me to dinner and told me to dress accordingly," I chuckled. "I thought it would be a small, private thing. I guess not. I better get going," I stood to leave. I still wanted to examine the carvings upstairs—and now I had to dress for a formal event, too.

"No, stay," Don urged.

"Alright, for a few more minutes," I agreed, taking my seat again.

Don nodded toward the book I was carrying and grinned. "Chapter 3 is the most fascinating part of that book."

"You have the entire volume memorized?" I laughed.

"More or less," he grinned. "Take these," Don urged, sliding two large keys across the table. "They unlock some things on the upper levels. I think you'll find the stuff there fascinating."

"Thanks," I nodded, slipping the keys into my pocket.

"Is this your first time here?" Don asked.

"Essentially."

"The path over there leads to a lake. It's more private. Lots of amazing fish," he confided. "I can show you something there later that would help with the book."

"Thanks," I smiled. "Help is always appreciated. I really better get going now." I stood up again.

"It's going to be amazing, Katharine," Don called after me as I walked toward the house.

"What's going to be amazing?" I shouted back, smiling. "The book? The earth? Salem's party?"

"All of it," he answered, grinning broadly.

Chapter 6

Hurrying down the hall, I noticed a familiar face coming towards me.

"Time!" I shouted. "What are you doing here?"

"The kings invited me," he answered. "How you relate to time is going to change dramatically in the new era. They wanted me to help explain the changes."

Talking about a spiritual being named "Time" can be confusing. There's an angel who calls himself Time who helps administer time for Yahweh. I had chatted with that angel a lot. But there's also a being who embodies the essence of time itself. I think of heavenly beings as the essence of something put in a form we can interact with. So the being Time is all the things that make up time—with a consciousness we can connect with and a form we can see.

It was the being Time who stopped to greet me now. "Do you have a second?" he asked. "I'd love to talk to you privately."

When I agreed, he unlocked a room just up the hallway. When I stepped into the small sitting room, I was overwhelmed by the clocks. A hundred clocks of all sizes and shapes filled the space. Most clocks were ticking loudly. There was even a large, gold metronome. As its pendulum swung back and forth methodically, a very loud clicking sounded. The room was so noisy with ticking that I was about to ask Time if he could find another room to chat in.

"This is the clockworks room of the King of Salem," Time announced.

"I thought it appropriate that we meet here."

I was intrigued. "I didn't know the king had a clockworks room."

"He most certainly does," Time answered with a nod. "What do you want to know about time?"

"Everything," I smiled.

"To show you everything, I may have to take you back to the Beginning," Time replied.

"I guess it would have to be the Beginning," I answered. "You didn't exist before then, did you?"

"Place your hand on the center of my chest," he commanded. "And I'll take you where you want to go."

HALLWAY OF TIME

When I complied, we weren't in the Beginning. We were standing in a long hallway with several doors on the right.

"We're in a place that I'm going to call, for the sake of the book, the Hallway of Time," he announced. "Open a few doors and tell me what you see."

I chose doors randomly. The first door opened to a world of dinosaurs. I quickly shut it. The next door revealed a formless void in the middle of the cosmos.

"These doors lead to different places," I told Time.

"No, they take you to the same place—in different epochs," Time explained. "You're seeing earth in different dispensations or ages or epochs. Look at the numbers above the doors."

For the first time, I noticed the doors were numbered one through thirteen, from right to left.

"Stand in front of the thirteenth door," he directed. Once I was in position, he continued. "You're about to open the door in the thirteenth age of earth's history," Time explained. "Not just in this hallway. All of earth is opening to it. You've heard it called different names, haven't you?"

"I've heard it called the Age of Aquarius (by people using the secular calendar) and the Age of Leo (by people using the biblical calendar). I've also heard people giving it no name at all. They just believe a new era with a higher level of consciousness is opening," I reported.

"Here, we're calling it the 13th Age. The blueprints for the new heaven and new earth are being released in the 13th Mountain. The group of people working with that Mountain call themselves the 13th Tribe. That's why you see the number thirteen above the door," Time explained.

"Why thirteen?" I wondered.

"Because the first twelve ages have already passed."

"But doesn't thirteen also mean something else?" I pressed. "There are twelve constellations in the night sky. The earth is in the center of those constellations. It's the thirteenth. There were twelve disciples in the New Testament, all centered around Jesus, who was the thirteenth. There were twelve tribes of Israel, all centered around Yahweh's presence in the Tabernacle. Then, the Bible talks about a tribe who served as a priest in that Tabernacle. But that tribe wasn't mentioned among the twelve—a tribe after the order of Melchizedek (Hebrews 7:13). That's the thirteenth.

"Isn't the thirteenth age the age that the twelve other ages point to, support, and surround? The thirteenth tribe is the tribe that fulfills the functions of the other tribes—but from our complete, eternal, limitless nature. We're the Jesus. The other ages and tribes were the disciples," I winked. "We're entering an age where every other epoch in earth's history has been pointing to. We're the fulfillment of it. We're the climax."

"Yes," Time replied. "You're at a point in history unlike any before it. Like the people who found a new nation, your generation is founding a new era for all the earth. You'll establish the government and structures that everything will flow from."

"We have the chance to write the laws to have cities named after us?"

I grinned.

"All of that and more," he said. "It's time. Open the door now, Katharine."

13TH DOOR

I'm not sure what I was expecting. But it certainly wasn't what I found. When I opened the door, a translucent being shining with pure, white light was floating about a foot off the ground.

"Welcome, Katharine!" she announced. "On behalf of everyone here who have been waiting and preparing for this day, we greet all of you in humanity arcing with us now. Your beam of light will arc with ours. Together, we open the new era."

"Who are you?" I asked.

"I'm a Guiding Light," she replied. "I'm not the only one of my kind. I've been preparing for this day. We're about to send an army of Guiding Lights so people can find the way here."

"You have a message for the book, don't you?" I sensed.

"Don't be afraid of the transition coming on earth. Yeshua called it the birth pangs. What you birth will be well worth it."

"What kinds of birth pangs should we expect?" I wondered.

"The things holding humanity back will be removed. They are mostly mindsets and structures—and the systems that have formed around those structures. You're removing those old structures from your life now. That's enabling you to step into the new era powerfully."

When she explained it like that, I understood. I was refusing to make the same decisions that the generations before me had made—decisions that religious structures called holy and righteous—but had ended in death. Several times, I sat in our mega-church, surrounded by a thousand Christians, and thought, "I could make choices every one of these people would applaud. They'd call me holy, amazing, wise. But all those labels would mean is that I lived under the same structure they did. I chose the same mindsets. And these mindsets have led generation after generation to death. These people may all die—despite living the best way their mindsets tell them to.

"Or I could live from a different mindset," I had thought, sitting in the mega-church. "I could flow with Holiness and Righteousness as they truly are—expressions of the divine nature that emanates from Yahweh's heart. I could flow with his heart and do something unbelievable for humanity. I could open something brand new. I'd be labeled a heretic. I'd be tossed out and pitied. But I would be living the reason I came to earth."

Long story short, I chose to be ridiculed and misunderstood to open a different ending for humanity. Death isn't our destiny. Life is. I've chosen Life.

Standing with Time at the threshold of the 13th door, I realized I had found others who had also chosen Life. And with people like Don and beings like the King of Salem, we finally had the power to manifest the Life humanity has longed for.

Chapter 7

When I finally returned to my room, there was no time to study the engravings book. Instead, I rushed to dress for the formal dinner. I chose a floor-length dark red evening gown covered with sparkly sequins. Matching red heels and a diamond necklace completed the outfit.

By the time I arrived downstairs, the party was in full swing. Countless guests milled through the rooms on the first floor. I was glad I had selected an elegant dress. Everyone was dressed like movie stars at the opening of a Hollywood blockbuster.

I wound through the crowd until I came to a room with mahogany bookshelves and a roaring fire. There, Salem approached me, cocktail in hand.

"Katharine!" he shouted cheerfully. "You don't have a drink. Let's remedy that." He immediately wandered off, presumably to find the perfect drink.

There was so much drinking at this event. It reminded me of parties Solomon threw. Speaking of Solomon, I looked up to find him standing in front of me, next to a gorgeous plus one.

"Good to see you, Katharine," he leaned over to kiss my cheek in greeting.

"Good to see you, too," I smiled.

"You're wondering why we're celebrating the opening of the 13th Mountain?" Solomon asked.

"Is that what this party is about?" I asked.

"Oh, yes. The three kings decided to open the King of Salem's house for festivities lasting three days. Do you know why?" Solomon didn't wait for a response. "When you celebrate something, you solidify it in reality. No one celebrates something that hasn't happened, right? You haven't had your 100th birthday party, have you? That's because you haven't reached 100 yet. But you have had your 10th birthday party. By celebrating the mountain's opening, we're proclaiming that it's here and open. We're making it even more accessible to people."

"That makes sense," I nodded thoughtfully.

"Celebrating also raises our moods," Solomon continued. "Then, when you interact with teachings about the 13th Mountain, you're in better spirits. You approach it differently. You can receive insights from a higher perspective."

"That also makes sense," I agreed. "But I was wondering why you celebrated with alcohol."

"You wonder what the wine that we're drinking stands for? In the natural world, alcohol makes the heart merry. It helps you overcome barriers to releasing yourself to others," Solomon answered. "It makes you feel more bonded to those here, doesn't it?"

"I suppose it does all those things," I mused.

"Ponder some scripture about it, Katharine, if you want to take it deeper," Solomon advised.

"Are you talking about all the drinking here?" Don asked good-naturedly as he joined the conversation. In his right hand, he was nursing a potent cocktail.

"It's a bit excessive, don't you think?" I asked, glancing at his drink and smiling.

"You know what wine stands for, don't you, Katharine?" he replied. "In the spiritual world, wine is the record of the glory of Yahweh seen in an individual's life. When you drink it, you experience the testimony of their intimate walk with Yahweh and how that was expressed through their life."

"So when Salem serves us his wine, we're taking into us a record of the glory of Yahweh that he embodies?" I clarified.

"Absolutely. Someone like Salem—or Solomon," Don nodded in greeting to the king beside him, "can offer you their wine. Or you can go to the wine room in the mountain of Yahweh. There, you'll find vats of the wine of every individual who's ever lived."

"Could I drink their wine there?" I wondered.

"Yes, if you're ready for it," Don answered.

"I understand the wine," I replied. "It's all the hard liquor that I don't get. Why is Salem pouring us mixed drinks?"

"Think about my writing, Katharine," Solomon offered. "Where do you see mixed drinks in the Bible?"

"It's in Song of Solomon," I mused.

"And Proverbs," Don added.

"You're both right," Solomon nodded. "In Proverbs, I wrote about how Wisdom built her house, mixed her wine, and set her table."

"Some translations call mixed wine 'liquor.' Is that why I'm seeing it as liquor?" I asked.

"Could be," Solomon replied. "In Proverbs 9, I talked about going to Wisdom's house and drinking her mixed wine."

"And you served the same kind of mixed wine—or liquor—at your banqueting table," I realized. "You talk about mixed wine being part of what you and your spouse drink in intimacy."

"In the spiritual realms, the hard liquor is the opiated stuff that sends you into greater encounters and understandings," Don explained. "We don't want to be crazy drunk or high in the natural world. But, in the spirit, the liquor is the meaty stuff that takes you into much wilder encounters."

"Just like in the natural world, opiates trip you out? They send you somewhere else," I mused. "So all this drinking is symbolic of meaty truths being revealed in our interactions here?"

"It's more than symbolic," Don answered. "It will take you places the wine alone won't. The normal wine is just a record. The mixed wine or liquor is meatier stuff."

"If that's the case, I'll drink a lot while I'm here," I laughed. "I want to get the most out of these encounters."

As if on cue, Salem returned with a drink for me. "Katharine, drink. Meet your new friends," he urged.

"Speaking of new friends, I'd like to introduce you to Rebekah," Solomon motioned to the stunning woman beside him. "She was one of my wives. Not the matriarch, Rebekah, of course. My Rebekah's name wasn't mentioned in the Bible. But she and I did a lot of interesting things together. She could show you some fascinating things."

"Pleasure to meet you," I smiled at the queen as Don nodded to acknowledge her.

"The pleasure is mine," she answered, kissing me briefly on the cheek in greeting. "Solomon asked me to organize the efforts of his wives."

"Rebekah is a master organizer," Solomon cut in. "She's also an expert in manifestation."

The queen smiled. "I can help you organize the people you work with as well as your staff," the queen offered. "We can make you more efficient and effective regarding manifestation."

"I welcome your help," I replied, smiling.

FRIENDS

As I looked around the room, I recognized a few people. Ian Clayton stood by the King of Righteousness and the King of Peace. They were all laughing loudly. It seemed fitting.

Continuing to sweep the room with my eyes, I noticed Enoch by the fire. Happy to see him, I quickly excused myself and hurried over to him.

"Good to see you, Katharine," he smiled, leaning over to kiss me on the cheek.

Was that the cultural norm here? I wondered. The Bible talks about greeting people with a holy kiss (2 Cor. 13:12). But I have never had so many people from heaven actually do that. Then, a thought occurred to me. In the Bible, kisses and wine do similar things—they transfer the record of someone's essence to you (Song of Sol. 1:2). (In intimacy, the queen longed for the king's kisses more than his wine. But they both intoxicated her with the record of who he is.) As 2 Corinthians 13:12 clarifies, kisses don't have to signal spousal intimacy. Even a quick peck on the cheek in greeting can impart something important. When I realized this, I smiled broadly at Enoch. I figured everyone here who greeted me with a holy kiss was transferring something about themselves that I needed right now.

"Be sure to talk to me later," Enoch winked. "I have something to tell you for the book."

"Absolutely."

"Enjoying your stay here?" he asked.

"It's been quite the experience," I replied.

I almost had to shout. There were so many conversations going on it was difficult to hear. Everyone who had a significant role in the 13th Mountain's release seemed to have been invited. With a plus one.

But it was one of the most enjoyable parties I had ever attended in the realms. It felt like the best kind of family reunion you could imagine. You could connect with people you had meaningful relationships with. But your relationships weren't a thing of the past. You weren't recounting old times—not mostly. You were celebrating what you were about to do together. The most important part of your connection lies ahead of you. Everyone was upbeat and ready to go.

As I talked with Enoch, Moshe caught my eye across the room. Smiling, he raised his glass to me. I did the same back. The energy of everyone in the room filled my heart with warm joy. I couldn't stop smiling.

BANQUET

Just then, the dinner bell rang. A dozen doors simultaneously opened as servants stepped out to welcome us into the dining area. Guests were ushered to assigned seating along three long tables. One of the three kings sat at the head of each table—the King of Salem, the King of Righteousness, and the King of Peace.

By the time I found my chair, nearly everyone else at the table had already been seated. To my surprise, I was seated immediately to the right of the King of Salem. I guess that's what you get when you're writing a book about him. As I sat down, I noticed Don was seated across from me.

Salem used dinner as an opportunity to speak to everyone present. He gave a moving speech about entering a new era for all creation. He urged everyone to take their part in forming the new heaven and new earth. He even called on a few people at the tables to share short insights and encouragements. There was such a full agenda during dinner that I barely spoke to the people at my table until dessert.

"Are you finding plenty of material for your book?" the king of Salem asked over our third glass of wine.

"Yes, sir. You have an amazing house. Full of mystery and knowledge. And you have important things going on here," I replied, thinking of Melchizedek's committee meeting. "Spending time here is well worth it. But I have a feeling your house's greatest treasure is you."

"And what makes you say that, Katharine?" he asked. The wine was making his spirits high.

"The greatest treasure about any glorious king is never something they possess, sir," I answered. "It's always who they are. I haven't dug deep enough yet to figure out how you amassed the wealth you did. I'm not sure how or why or even when you built your city I've heard so much about. But I guarantee you that you were able to do those things only because they are a reflection of what's inside you. People build from the inside out. The greatest thing you can teach us—the biggest treasure you can release to the world—isn't found in your storehouses. It's not in your libraries. It's inside there, sir," I said, nodding towards his heart. "I've seen a bit of what's inside you. And I would come back here if this place were a hovel—just to get to know what's inside you," I smiled.

"Well said, Katharine," Salem smiled with tender appreciation. "I welcome you to come back anytime to get to know who I am and not just what I do," he added. "But I promise you I'll treat you like a queen. No hovels here."

I laughed.

"Now, if you'll excuse me, I have some host duties to attend to," Salem addressed all of us as he rose from the table.

COMPANIONS

I chatted pleasantly with the woman next to me for several minutes. Then Don cleared his throat loudly. When I glanced at him, he said, "Do you want to explore? People are leaving the dinner tables."

"Sure," I replied, taking leave of the woman to my right.

We wandered aimlessly for a while, swapping stories about who we had talked to before dinner. When we came to an alcove in the back of a study, Don told me, "Stay here. I'll be right back with some drinks."

"Sure," I laughed, even though I had drunk so much already. After the talk with Solomon about what the wine stood for, I wouldn't refuse a drink—at least not in these visions.

When Don took longer than expected, I did what made the most sense. I began to work. When he returned, I was deep in conversation with two women.

"If I had known you'd have two remarkable friends with you, I would have brought more drinks," Don smiled, handing over a champagne glass.

"I was reviewing notes with two of my staff," I answered, accepting the champagne. "When I realized this was a formal state event and not a personal trip, I asked some of my staff to join me," I explained. "Don, meet two of my staff members—Clarity and Wisdom."

Don nodded respectfully.

"She's not the spirit of Wisdom, of course," I explained. "She's a representation of my own wisdom, especially as it applies to my work. I wanted these companions to join me as I experience things for the book."

"Very wise," Don winked. I couldn't tell if he was making a pun or not.

My staff curtsied to him reverentially.

"You may go now," I told them. "I'd like to speak with the king by myself."

AMBASSADORS

"Let's mingle," Don suggested as he motioned for us to move deeper into the crowd. "So many fascinating people to meet."

"Fascinating is one word for it. Look at who's in this room. You'd think we were at a cast party for Star Wars. I've never seen so many other worldly creatures in one place."

Don chuckled. "They are the ambassadors from their species here to celebrate the opening of the 13th Mountain," he explained. "What will come from this mountain will be important far beyond earth. It will touch everything in creation. Many of these ambassadors will work with us to spread the technologies we develop to their own kind."

"I know," I nodded. "I met one of the ambassadors at my home on earth not long ago. For his species, at least, it was an honor to be picked as a liaison with humanity. It was a very tough selection process, he told me."

"Interesting," Don remarked.

"Yes. I saw some of what's in him. And that gave me greater respect for all these representatives. They tried to pick the most mature, brightest of their species to interface with us," I reported. "His love for humanity ran deep."

As we talked, we passed the main ballroom. One of its double doors was open, revealing a spacious dance floor. Inside, beings of all sorts were twirling around in formal attire. A live orchestra played in perfect pitch. Hearing just a few notes nearly sent me into ecstasy.

"Salem really knows how to throw a party," I sighed. "He didn't pull any stops."

"No," Don laughed. "But I think you'll find what's planned for the back patio the most fascinating part of the evening."

"Really? How do you know?" I asked. "Were you on the planning committee or something?"

I was joking. But when he didn't answer, I wondered if he was.

SPECIAL GUEST

We stepped onto the patio where we had sat with Holiness and Righteousness earlier. Now, tiny lights were strung everywhere. Their twinkling accented the stars in the pitch-black night sky. It gave the place a breathtaking feel.

Another live band was playing on a stage in front of the bay windows that peered into the library. A few couples were swaying to the music on the stone pavers in front of the makeshift stage.

Nodding, Don directed my attention to the stage. "Not the music," he whispered, smiling knowingly. "Her."

As he spoke, the musicians stopped playing while a stunning being walked to center stage.

"Abundance," Don whispered.

"I've been asked to say a few words tonight," the being began. "Your host wanted to save the best part of the evening for last. He said that's how Yahweh planned everything to happen, too. So I want to share a message with each of you."

I saw it coming. When she spoke the last words, a wave of energy flowed from her, disrupting everything in its wake. Like a movie played in slow motion, I saw the wave distorting the airwaves around it as it moved closer and closer and—

The next thing I knew, I was on the ground. The wave had knocked me over as it passed through me. I wasn't sure if it moved Don back a few inches, but it didn't knock him over. Quickly, he extended his hand to help me up.

Looking around, I realized most people on the patio were like Don— unshaken. Some were like me, knocked over but unharmed. A few people had gotten knocked down and were injured. Perhaps they were dead. Medics were called to revive them.

"Why were they invited when they could be so easily injured by what happens here?" I asked Don, alarmed.

"Don't worry. They'll be fine," he assured. "The imagery of the medics is just to show you how powerful the communication wave from Abundance was. She transmitted a different message to each person. Your message will be for the book."

"It was one of those heavenly ways to communicate?" I asked.

DREAM

Right after that, I fell asleep—on earth. While sleeping, I had a dream showing me the message Abundance told me. When I woke up on earth, I was still in the vision. Don and a few people I didn't recognize stood over me, ensuring I was okay after my fall. I was eager to share my dream.

"I had a dream about the liberation of South America from Spanish rule," I began, animated. "There, liberators fought for the freedom of the entire continent—not just their own country. For example, Bernardo

O'Higgins is considered the liberator of Chile. But he also held the highest rank in the armies of several other nations."

"How do you know all that, Katharine?" Don interrupted, amused.

"I studied this stuff in school," I answered. "After the battles, South America has never been ruled by an outside power. The liberators ushered in a new, permanent era. Abundance showed me it's time for the world to be liberated from what's held it in bondage. We're slaves to things like death, poverty, and brokenness. Liberators who will bring freedom from these things to the whole world will arise. Their work won't be limited to one country or one people group. They will fight to end the bondage the entire world has been subject to. And guess what new era these liberators will usher in?"

"What?" Don asked, smiling.

"Abundance," I answered. "We'll have abundant life, abundant provision, abundant joy—just to name a few. The world will never go back to how it was before. Right now, liberators are being recruited. It's time to start. We're at a point in history where our work will be celebrated for generations because it will usher in a new era for humanity."

Don was standing next to my chair. As I looked up at him, his form opened so I could see into who he is as a spirit being. Countless hosts of armies were inside him, lined up, as glorious as the stars. All his armies were ready to march into battle. It reminded me of a verse in Song of Solomon describing the queen: "Who is this, arising like the dawn, as fair as the moon, as bright as the sun, as majestic as an army with billowing banners?" (Song of Sol. 6:10 NLT).

His armies felt powerful enough to liberate creation all by themselves. What if he worked next to others like him? Nothing could stop all of creation from being permanently, completely changed!

I was thinking about all this, but didn't speak it out loud. I must have been staring at him blankly.

"Katharine, are you okay?" Don asked, concerned. "Should I call a medic?"

"No, no. I'm alright," I insisted. "I was just realizing what the people who build the new heaven and new earth will look like."

INTENTIONS

Don pulled up a chair and sat down. "I think you should rest here a bit longer—just to be sure."

Most people had gone in for the evening. The crowd had thinned out a lot. But the band had started playing again. A few people were dancing on the stone pavers, laughing loudly.

As we watched the couples dancing, Don asked, "Do you know my intentions for this book?"

"You have intentions for my book?" I replied, astonished.

"I have intentions for everything I think about, even if my intentions are in my spirit being, not my mind," he replied.

"I hadn't thought to read your intentions for this book," I confessed.

"Do it now," he suggested. "Read me. What do I intend for this book?"

"Let's see," I smiled, closing my eyes to concentrate. "You want to impart knowledge and understanding about how we can build the new heaven and new earth. You want to release some things that we'll need to do that. But your biggest objective is to call people to their full identity," I reported. "You want more people to fully embrace who we are—and live it completely."

"Not bad," Don smiled.

"I'm not done. You want to have fun writing the book." I opened my eyes briefly to grin at him. "You want to get to know Yahweh better—his splendor and glory."

"Well done," Don nodded.

"There's more. I see Visions, like a being, with us for this book. She's a companion," I reported.

"Like Holiness and Righteousness accompanied me?" Don asked.

"Yes, and Clarity and Wisdom came at my request," I nodded. "Visions is here in response to both of our hearts. She will release clearer, higher-level visions for the readers," I explained. "And I hope for me, too," I added quickly. "These visions have been clearer for me."

"That's good," Don replied. "Some amazing things are going to be released."

I opened my eyes, signaling that I was done reading his intentions. We grew silent for a moment, breathing in the fresh, perfect air at Salem's place. Then we started chatting about what the next couple of days may hold. Before long, I realized how late it was getting.

"I want to dive into the book about engravings tonight," I told Don. "So I better get going. It was enlightening to interact with you today, as always. I'm sure we'll run into each other tomorrow. Good night."

"It's going to be amazing, Katharine," Don called over his shoulder.

"What's going to be amazing? My night? Salem's party? The entire earth?" I shouted back.

"All of it," Don replied, smiling broadly.

Chapter 8

Half an hour had passed from the time I returned to my room. I had hastily dressed for bed, slipping on the first nightgown I found in the well-stocked closet. But I didn't slide under the covers. Instead, I sat at the desk, studying the book I had borrowed from Salem's library. I was immersed in its depths when I heard a knock on the door.

Hesitantly, I opened the door a crack. It was Don. "What are you doing here?" I whispered. He was dressed entirely in black.

"Someone swore he couldn't wait until tomorrow to see you," Don grinned, pushing the door open a few more inches. Now, I could see a familiar figure standing next to Don.

"Moshe!" I beamed. "It's so good to see you!"

"The excitement is all mine," he grinned. Quickly, he gave me a half hug and kiss on the cheek. He, too, was dressed all in black.

"What's with the black? Are you two breaking into the vault?" I smiled. "Come on in."

"No, we came to invite you to join us," Moshe replied. "There's a hidden treasure here I promised to show Don. I want to show you, too. Grab the keys Don gave you and come with us."

"Plus, I brought this," Don smiled, holding up a bottle of Salem's wine and three glasses.

I hesitated momentarily. Then I was all in. "Alright. Let me get dressed."

"No, we don't have time for that," Don insisted. "What you're wearing is fine."

I glanced at my outfit. "There's no way I'm going with the two of you unless I'm also dressed all in black. I can't ruin the team's stealth-mode dynamics," I winked.

Two minutes later, I was dressed like my co-explorers, holding the keys Don had given me earlier. As we started down the hall, I felt like I was on a top-secret mission with two universe-renowned undercover agents to unearth national treasures—or perhaps intergalactic treasures—that could save the cosmos.

Despite the adrenaline rush, I began to have second thoughts as we climbed to the third floor. "Are you sure we're allowed to sneak around Salem's house in the middle of the night, drinking wine from his private stash?"

"I am absolutely positive that he wouldn't mind if he found out," Don replied.

"That's not exactly what I asked," I pointed out.

"No one's going to see us anyway," Moshe remarked. "Everyone knows that wearing all black makes you undetectable."

Instinctively, my mind searched for Bible verses to unlock a deeper spiritual truth to Moshe's comment. Then I decided maybe he was just being funny. But I wasn't 100 percent sure. I figured everything coming from Moshe's mouth might contain a higher truth.

SECRET PASSAGE

We wound through Salem's halls in silence. When we came to a particular hallway on the third floor, the men paused in front of a wall. Like most of the walls, it had hand-carved engravings wound through the molding.

"Here," Moshe announced. "Press this part of the engraving."

When I did, a secret passage opened. Dust spurted out, covering all of us. But the dust was the least of our concerns. The passage itself was overgrown with thick cobwebs. I had never seen cobwebs as hefty as these. To most people, they would have blocked the passage. But not to Don and Moshe.

"We're going in there?" I grimaced.

"Absolutely," Don replied. "The greatest treasures are often the ones most difficult to uncover."

"I trust you that this will be worth it," I announced, taking a deep breath and plunging after them.

We were ascending a long, narrow staircase. Even though Moshe and Don were taking the brunt of the cobwebs, they were so abundant that I frequently had cobwebs in my mouth and up my nose, making it difficult to breathe. We had to stop periodically and de-web ourselves.

About half way up, I asked, "You're sure this will be worth it?"

"Forerunners pave the way, Katharine. They pay a price," Moshe answered. "Those who follow us won't face the obstacles we did. But there's a reward for path-making. So, yes, it will be worth it."

"How did you know about this secret passage anyway?" I asked.

"I told Don about this passage not long ago," Moshe answered. "I discovered it myself in an earlier epoch."

"I believe that. It's been a long time since anyone's been in this passage," I replied.

Moshe chuckled. Or, at least, I thought the sound coming from his throat was a chuckle. He may have been coughing up a spiderweb. They were so abundant. Finally, we reached the top of the staircase.

We were all covered from head to toe in dust and cobwebs. For several minutes, we de-webbed ourselves. Despite our best efforts, our completely black outfits were now completely white. It wasn't anything a good washing couldn't solve. But until then, Moshe would need to joke about being hidden in light rather than darkness. We were much closer to balls of white light than black clouds.

THE ATTIC

"Put the key in this lock," Moshe directed, swooshing cobwebs away from the handle. With a loud creak, the door opened. "I present to you one of the hidden attic chambers of the King of Salem," he announced ceremoniously.

At least it wasn't filled with cobwebs. But a thick layer of dust covered everything. Don eagerly began exploring. I joined him.

"Anything in particular we're looking for?" I asked.

"There are several priceless artifacts here," Moshe replied.

"Look at this. Candles of Illumination," Don announced as he found the first treasure. "These are rare. If you study a book under the light of one of these candles, you'll understand things in a deeper light. Take some for your studies, Katharine."

"Can we just take something from Salem's attic?" I questioned.

"You're on the Distribution Committee. Can't you decide to distribute these to yourself?" Don suggested, grinning.

"I am not on the Distribution Committee," I answered, laughing. "And, even if I was, the committee asks people to lend items to the public library voluntarily. We don't raid people's houses, taking whatever we want."

"I guarantee you he wants you to have them. Ask him tomorrow. Then give them back if he says no," Don suggested matter-of-factly.

"Oh, alright. Give me a couple."

TWICE HIDDEN

"Some of the greatest treasures lie below the surface level," Don explained as we continued searching the attic. "Don't stop at the first level of understanding that unfolds to you. Look deeper, and more will open."

"Like how you taught me to stand with Understanding and look at any encounter or revelation again—through his eye?" I asked.

"Yes, even after you've unlocked something hidden—like this attic—there are treasures concealed deeper," Don explained.

"There certainly are," Moshe agreed. "There's a floorboard that opens right around here—"

For a minute, he pressed his feet in several spots until, with a creak, a board sprang up. Hurrying over, I knelt on the dusty floor, excitement racing through me. What treasure had been hidden twice?

Kneeling beside me, Don pulled out an ancient glass bottle, elegantly crafted. "Is this what I think it is?" he asked excitedly. Opening the bottle, he spilled some of its contents into his hand. "Manifestation seeds," he announced triumphantly.

With the jar in his hand, his power to manifest was drawn to the surface. Waves of it emanated from him and hit Moshe and me. Grinning, I told Don, "Your ability to create is radiating out from you so powerfully that it's overwhelming me—and about five other dimensions. What's so special about those seeds?"

Don laughed as Moshe explained, "These seeds don't hold ordinary abilities to manifest. They can create anything—anything at all."

"Do you know what happens when you can create anything at all?" Don asked excitedly.

"They call you God?" I joked.

"Each of you should eat one of these seeds," Moshe directed, shoving a seed into my hand.

"Shouldn't we plant a seed, not eat it?" I questioned.

"The best soil for this kind of seed is the soil of the heart," Moshe winked.

So, as Moshe watched, Don and I both swallowed a huge seed.

"Feel it inside you, Katharine—the ability to create anything. It's in seed form now. You'll awaken to it and grow it inside you. So will the readers who apply themselves to it."

"Thanks, Moshe," I smiled.

"For what?"

"For all of it. But right now, I'm thanking you for this manifestation seed and for what you're doing in creation. I know you hold a key to building the new heaven and new earth. Thanks for sharing what you've unlocked with us."

"My pleasure," he smiled before returning to rummaging around the attic.

I stood silently for a minute, watching the men explore the treasure trove. Both of them were enjoying themselves immensely. Moshe looked like a scholar returning to an old study, reconnecting with forgotten treasures. From the look on Don's face, you'd think we were in a bank while they were handing out free money. Maybe the attic was like that— only better.

THE BOOK

"Here is it," Moshe announced a minute later, holding up a rectangular green book covered in dust. "This is what I wanted to show you. It's one of the priceless treasures hidden here."

"What is it?" I asked, my excitement building.

"Open it and find out," he directed, handing me the book.

Don paused from his exploration to glance at what I was holding. A look of recognition crossed his face. He smiled.

I found a spot under the attic's nearest window. Moonlight was pouring through, illuminating a rectangular area on the floor. Sitting on the dusty wooden planks, I opened the book with reverent expectation.

There were words written on the page. But I didn't read the words. The words spoke. In a thunderous voice, they uttered the sounds that their markings tried to capture. I had studied Hebrew in seminary. Then, I memorized part of Genesis 1 in Hebrew. So, I knew exactly what the words were saying.

"These are the words Yahweh spoke at creation," I announced, awe in my voice. "Were those words recorded in a living book? Are we hearing the actual voice of God as he formed everything?"

"Wow," Don whistled, filled with awe. Slowly, he sat beside me on the floor as Moshe stood over us.

"Open the book again," Moshe directed.

So, I closed the volume and reopened it to the first page. Again, it spoke the words, just as before. This time, as the voice boomed, it transported us into the voice. We were floating in its frequency, feeling every change in pitch, being penetrated by every beam of light encasing the sound. It felt like we had been broken into billions of tiny waves—sound waves. We were encased at a microscopic or quantum level in the waves of Yahweh's voice.

As his voice traveled into the farthest reaches of what existed, we were stretched out along with it. The longer we floated in that entanglement, the more of Yahweh penetrated us. Deep inside, we could feel what Yahweh was thinking and feeling as he spoke the words of creation. His heart, his character, and his essence were open and laid bare to us.

The intensity of the experience increased with each moment we stayed in it. Yet time had no meaning. I wasn't sure if we peered into Yahweh, entangled with his voice, for seconds, days, or millennia. But the longer I stayed, the more frightening it became.

I think it was my body who pulled me out. It was shaking violently as waves of terror overwhelmed me. But my mind was equally terrified. I lay on the attic floor, convulsing uncontrollably, afraid for my life. When the violent shaking wouldn't let up, I wondered if I may actually die.

The men must have grown alarmed, too. They opened themselves up, encasing us with the light of their essence. At the same time, strong arms that felt like Yahweh's grabbed me fiercely from behind. They held me tightly as wave after wave of terror rattled my body. The light and the strength encasing me absorbed the brunt of the terror as it swept through me. After several long minutes, the shaking began to subside.

My body was only slightly trembling. But my mind was still racing with fright. I sat on the floor, stunned and silent.

"I almost died," I whispered. "But I saw him."

"So did we," Moshe and Don spoke simultaneously in low tones.

"And he saw me," I said. "I didn't know I could see or be seen like that. Everything was opened and laid bare."

"I know," Moshe spoke comfortingly.

"I'm so scared," I confessed. "It was the most terrifying and most wonderful thing I've ever experienced."

"You're okay now," Moshe told me reassuringly.

"If we had done that on earth, do you think I would have died?" I asked. "It was a vision within a vision, and I'm still so scared."

"Don't ask yourself questions like that, Katharine," Don answered. "Yahweh's not going to let you die."

"Do you think we were really there? When his voice created everything, were we entangled with it? Does everything that exists have our essence woven into it?" I asked. "I teach that we were in Yahweh's spirit at creation because he hadn't breathed his spirit into humanity yet. So we were still one with him. So I believed that I was there. But I had never thought of it like I was entangled with the sound of his voice."

Slowly, the feeling of terror lifted, and I could remember the beautiful parts of the experience more clearly. My body began to tingle with delight (as well as tremble in terror every so often). To see him, to know him, was truly delightful.

"I feel like he saw me and accepted me. And I accepted him," I told them. "There was nothing hidden."

"There are some experiences too holy to describe in words," Don replied. "But I'll share with you what happened to me. It demands to be shared."

He opened himself up so we could peer inside. I saw Yahweh interfacing with Don in the Beginning. I heard Yahweh say, "Son, I give you this." Then he downloaded the blueprints he used to create everything into Don.

"Wow," I whispered. "The feeling of that moment was like a father handing the keys of the family business to his son. He was acknowledging that you were capable and trustworthy enough to begin leading the family business. I think he expects you to do more with it than he did— like a father hopes his son will expand the glory and treasures of the family business beyond where he took it. He's doing that with creation. That's the family business he gave you the keys to," I announced. The emotions Yahweh felt when he gave Don the blueprints hit me, filling me with holy awe.

"Yes," Don agreed, the same awe filling him.

"You stayed in the Beginning. Yahweh took me to the end," I told the men. "I saw myself taking a seat on a throne next to him. I was entirely glowing in light. He showed me the moment I fully matured into my divine nature and sat next to him as a sovereign peer."

THE WINE

Realizing I was still shaken, Moshe suggested we take out Salem's wine. "There's nothing like a good glass of wine after a terrifying encounter."

"I'll have to remember that," I laughed.

Still sitting on the floor, I leaned against a dust-covered desk as Moshe poured three generous glasses. "Tell me what you think of this vintage. I picked a very old one from his collection. It was from when he was still building his city, trading to amass his fortune."

The wine tasted very heavy to me. I could almost taste heavy metals in it.

"You're tasting his building materials," Moshe explained. "Things like gold and silver and bronze are what he used to build his city. Drinking this wine imparts an ability to build. There are things you need to build,

Katharine, on earth and in heaven. That's why I chose this wine."

I sipped the wine slowly, letting it reset my nerves. From my position leaning against the desk, I had a stunning view through the window. The moon was shimmering on a lake behind the estate, surrounded by a sky full of stars.

As the wine and the moon calmed me, I began to treasure the experience with the book more than be terrified by it.

"Those sounds we entangled with carry the blueprint for everything that exists, don't they?" I asked. "From those sounds, that light, those letters–anything can be formed."

"There's much more I can tell you, but not now. Just rest now," Moshe replied. "I want you two to have that book. We'll ask Salem for permission to remove it, of course. But this is a real treasure. It's why I wanted to take you to this attic tonight."

"There's a reason the book was rediscovered now," Don added. "It wanted to interact with us. It's time for humanity to create some things. And technologies like this will help us do it."

"You were both right," I confessed. "That book was worth eating cobwebs and being smothered in uncomfortableness. It's a terrifyingly wonderful treasure. And the greatest treasures are worth tracking down—no matter the cost. Are there more treasures on the caliber of that book here?"

"Without a doubt. Salem's collection is practically unparalleled," Don answered.

"We ought to come back and catalog it all—for the Distribution Committee. Or have some of our staff do it," I suggested. "We should at least know what's here. I'm leaning back against this desk—it's alive, right? It's communicating with me. It's the desk Salem used when he was building his city. The amount of knowledge in this desk alone is overwhelming. It contains secrets about how to trade, do business, and build kingdoms."

"Yeah, I sense that, too," Don agreed. "Everything we touch in here is alive with knowledge."

MORNING

I was still too shaken to want to return to my room. The thought of being alone in a strange house didn't fill me with warm fuzzies. So, I was content to keep chatting and sipping wine in the dusty attic. At least I felt safe there.

The next thing I knew, I was waking up. The wine bottle was empty. The moon had disappeared. My cobweb-filled hair was perched clumsily against the desk. But most alarmingly, sunlight was streaming through the window.

"Is it morning?" I asked groggily.

"Morning was due a few hours after we entered this place," Moshe answered. "So, yes, it's morning."

"Where's Don?" I wondered, looking around.

"You're the only one who dozed off. Don left when you fell asleep. But I didn't have the heart to wake you—or to leave you," Moshe answered.

"Thanks," I replied, yawning. "We need to hurry."

"We have time, Katharine," Moshe answered calmly. "You always have time. I want to say something to you privately. That's another reason I stayed when Don left."

I sat up straight up, combing my hair with my fingers in a futile attempt to look presentable before one of the most revered people in the Bible.

"I'm glad to be included in your little adventure," he said as genuine gratitude and excitement flowed from him. "I'm more excited about it than I can express right now. You think the creation book is important. And it is. But the book you're writing now will touch many lives. I'm glad to be part of it."

If I couldn't feel the excitement streaming from him, I would have found it hard to believe that the person who penned the first five books of the Bible—the best-selling book of all time—would be excited about being in this book. But his sentiments were real.

"I feel honored that you feel that way, Moshe," I replied, touching his face briefly in appreciation.

Without words, his essence spoke a thousand things to me in five seconds. "You'll know me in ways different from Don," he whispered. "That's why I wanted to catch a moment with you alone."

I'm not sure how long Moshe thought a moment was supposed to last. But that was the longest, most incredible moment I had spent with him in a while.

\

Day 2

Chapter 9

I missed breakfast. But, thankfully, Salem had counted on some people sleeping in. I'm not sure he had counted on people sneaking into his secret attic and falling asleep in the moonlight. But he had arranged for a table filled with breakfast food to be available till late morning. I was just in time.

In the hallways, hundreds of people and beings from all over the universe were milling around, waiting for the day's activities to begin. Munching on a croissant reserved for the late risers, I found a packet on the table with my name on it. Inside was a schedule for the day. The three kings had planned something like a conference. There were workshops, lectures, special lunches, group tours, and committee meetings. Everyone seemed to have a personalized schedule.

As I was examining my itinerary, Don walked up.

"Good morning," I smiled and yawned at the same time. "So now I know you abandon people who fall asleep."

"Are you kidding? Moshe practically shoved me out the door last night. Or this morning. Or whenever that was," Don answered. "He insisted on sitting in vigil over you all by himself."

I nodded, smiling. "Did you find your packet? What are you doing today?"

"My schedule is mostly meetings," Don replied. "How about you?"

"I have a one-on-one meeting with Salem," I answered. "But other than that, it's all lectures. I guess I'm in the stage of getting to know all this stuff."

"That's a good stage to be in," Don replied cheerfully. He was nodding to several people I didn't recognize as they passed us in the hall. "Has anyone offered to guide you through all this? I know it can be a bit overwhelming the first time in."

"I'm on my own, but I think I can manage," I smiled.

"I could come with you today," Don suggested. "I could sit in on the lectures with you and walk you through it. You'd get a lot more out of it that way. Not only for you—for the readers, too."

"When you put it like that—I'd be a horrible author to refuse your offer. But what about your meetings?"

"I could be in both places," he answered.

"Right, you can bilocate in the realms as easily as you can breathe," I remembered. "I'd love the help understanding things—as long as you can still attend your meetings."

"It's settled then," he replied. "What's your first lecture?"

"I want to take a look at the master list," I told him, grabbing a schedule from a nearby table. "The ones in my packet are just the ones suggested for me. I want to see everything they're offering."

A quick glance revealed an impressive line-up. The kings had divided the conference into topics relevant to the new era. In one wing of the house were lectures on mathematics, for example. All day, talks from people like Copernicus and Einstein explained the principles needed for a deeper grasp of various concepts. Others gave lectures on topics like inventions, travel, time, immortality, oneness, and finance.

"Don, you're one of the lecturers!" I gasped. "You didn't tell me."

"I just found out," he replied, smiling.

"I'm going to your lecture," I announced. "I want to witness you opening who you are to those here. You know it's not just people on earth you'll be speaking to. Being from all regions of the cosmos will be present. Everyone here will play a major role in unpacking the blueprints of the new heaven and new earth. And you were chosen to lecture to them. That's a huge deal. I'm including your lecture in the book."

FINANCE

Before he could answer, an important-looking figure rushing down the hall bumped into us. The papers he was carrying flew in every direction. As we all bent over to pick them up, he realized who we were.

"Don!" the being Finance greeted him warmly. "Katharine! Good to see you here." He looked at me quizzically for a moment. "Katharine, you're writing a book!"

How did he know?, I wondered. Looking down at myself, I noticed an official pen in my hand. Was that his signal?

"Walk with me for a moment," he told us. "I want to say something to you. I'm hurrying to my first lecture."

Side by side, we walked briskly down the main hallway. As people dodged around us, Finance spoke. "The opening of the 13th Mountain will bring a total change to finance, as you both know. Katharine, how you teach people to approach finance is opening the new era to them. Your heart for money—in all its components—and how you teach people to align to and love finance is crucial. I love your group, by the way," Finance leaned around Don to look at me directly. "You have the foundation. Don has the higher principles, shrouded in mystery now. Without those principles released, finance will not be revolutionized. But without the teaching Katharine is giving, no one will be able to accept the mysteries when they are revealed. You're working hand-in-hand even if you don't realize it. Katharine, listen to Don's wisdom. Don, don't disregard what Katharine's doing. Without it, people will not be ready for your stuff." Finance paused. "That's all I wanted to say for now. Good day to you both." With that, he ducked into the lecture hall.

"What was that all about?" Don asked quizzically.

"I'm leading what I call a Financial Boot Camp," I replied, blushing slightly. "I don't think I've mentioned it to you. It's not the deeper revelation you've unlocked about finances. But it probably is some of the foundations necessary to operate in finance in the new era. We're realigning ourselves with finance, clearing out limiting mindsets in our family lines, learning to approach finance through divine love, and meeting different beings related to finance. We're getting people's personal financial teams—in the spiritual realm—up and running. And we're aligning our identity, as it relates to finances, with our divine nature.

"I look at maturity in the next age as coming into our divine identity in every area of our lives," I continued. "Financial mastery isn't a skill set. It's an area in which we can grow into maturity. So, we aim to mature our divine identity in finance. I bet Finance is right. Without that kind of work, no one will be able to fully digest the higher teachings you have."

"Fascinating," Don nodded.

Chapter 10

Don and I hurried to the first lecture. Salem had dedicated at least a dozen rooms for lectures, so multiple topics were being discussed simultaneously. Slipping into the room, we found seats near the back. The room had fifty to seventy-five of the plushest conference chairs I had ever sat in. About half of them were filled.

The lecturer took a human-looking form. But he wasn't human. The kings had invited some beings from various dimensions and realms to lecture at the conference. These beings had knowledge that would be crucial in helping us build the new heaven and new earth.

"Good morning. You can call me Alfred," the lecturer began. "That's a close translation of my name's meaning into your language."

"Alfred means 'magical council,'" I whispered to Don. "Or simply 'wise.'"

Alfred was dressed in a long, flowing robe that stretched to the floor. Its thick, purple threads highlighted the honor he was being given here. But the clothes didn't have the regal feel of the three kings or Melchizedek.

"The earth has an enormously important role in restoring the cosmos," Alfred began. "Without humanity arising to its full potential, all creation will continue to wither. That's why those who do not want to rise to the true potential of humanity will be purged from the earth soon. They will choose to leave. Circumstances will force them on. Don't worry about them. They will be well cared for. Yahweh has made provisions for them. Their journey is not over. But the journey for the rest of humanity is about to begin.

"The earth will blossom until it becomes the—" Alfred's lecture stopped using words and began using images. He showed us a picture of the earth emitting brilliant light shining into the cosmos. Its "factories"— centers of knowledge and majesty—towered so high they reached into space. Earth had become the catalyst for something similar to the Industrial Revolution for the entire universe. The "smoke" from the factories was radiant light that fueled the cosmos. Just like the Industrial Revolution brought a new level of technology and progress for the whole planet, this cosmic Industrial Revolution will pull all creation to new levels. And earth will lead the way.

Alfred's lecture had begun with words. It had switched to images. And now it moved entirely to feelings that he conveyed to our hearts. I could feel how urgent it was that earth take its appointed role. My heart stirred, wanting to be part of it myself. I felt how crucial it was that everyone accept their roles. And I felt that things were happening now. Alfred's message wasn't a prophecy. It was a call to action. The game was beginning. It was the perfect time to join the team.

BODY

My body began tingling delightfully in response to Alfred's lecture. Don noticed.

"You're tingling and high, aren't you?" Don grinned.

"Yes," I smiled. "But that's the way it should be. The new heaven and new earth aren't just about better technology or endless life or abundance. It's also about feeling amazing. Who wants to live forever trapped in a decaying body and a miserable mind? Heaven isn't a location. It's a state of being.

"Have you heard people who have near-death experiences talk about how they went to heaven for a few minutes? They talk about how everything felt different in heaven. The atmosphere was filled with love or joy or peace, they'll report. But they'll say it wasn't like the love, joy, or peace on earth. It was a thousand times more intense, more delightful, more wonderful. That's how it will feel to live on earth. When we bring the feelings of heaven to earth, then we've really created heaven there. So, I welcome my body to feel amazing in response to touching heaven. I've trained it to open to what's going on spiritually. I want it to participate fully with the rest of me."

"I like that," Don replied.

"You do the same thing," I laughed. "I can feel how high you are sometimes. You're usually higher than I am. You can't unlock this stuff and not have it make you feel like the best day of your life is happening every day."

Don laughed, nodding in agreement.

FAITH

Alfred's lecture was over. People were beginning to leave the small room. Don and I were still in our seats, chatting.

"Do you want me to look inside you and see if anything is blocking you from moving into what Alfred was discussing?" Don asked. "Some people hear a teaching. They agree with it. They are even excited about it. But they fail to move into it because something is blocking them from taking it deep. I can check for you if you want me to."

"Yes, please do," I nodded.

He grew silent for a moment. Then he announced, "You have some doubt, Katharine."

"That doesn't surprise me," I sighed. "Sometimes, I wonder if I'll really enter into all of this. I keep thinking about a retired pastor I spoke to once. He'd been personally mentored by someone who teaches internationally about immortality. He hosted—maybe even spoke at— conferences like this one. He had all sorts of wild experiences in the spirit. And you know what he told me? He said he wasn't sure he wanted to be immortal because his body wasn't feeling good. How can someone who knows about all this—who's taught about it—how can they fail to enter in? How can they not even want to enter? And how can I know I won't have the same reaction?"

"It's because he didn't mix what he heard with faith," Don replied. "That's why he didn't enter the things he had tasted. Remember how, in the Bible, an entire generation of people who came out of slavery in Egypt didn't enter the promised land? The book of Hebrews explains why. It says they heard Yahweh's voice speaking at Mount Sinai," Don paused, raising his eyebrows and looking at me. I knew he was remembering last night. "They witnessed Yahweh's miracles. But they didn't mix what they saw and heard with faith."

"So they were scared of the giants and refused to fight for their inheritance," I finished his thought.

"Exactly. That's not what you're doing, Katharine," Don spoke confidently. "You're treating doubt like a foreign substance. It's like a virus that you conquer and rid yourself of. Other doubts may arise later. But you get rid of those, too. You're not harboring doubts. You have faith."

"There are giants here, you know," I sighed again. "Opening things like immortality and abundance for the earth has obstacles that appear to be insurmountable. But with faith, those giants seem like an afternoon snack—and not like a formidable foe."

"Exactly," Don nodded, animated. "Do you know why you have a huge reserve of faith deep inside you—a reserve so vast it will carry you into the promised land?"

"Why?" I asked, smiling that he was so confident I'd enter.

"Because you had several things in your life that forced you to develop faith. You believed for some things in faith, didn't you?" he pressed.

"Yes, but those things didn't happen," I confessed. "I had faith for years—against all odds—and then it didn't happen. Eventually, I stopped believing for it. I moved on. I thought it was a huge failure."

"It was anything but a failure," Don insisted. "Your faith opened a path to those things you wanted, even if it was through another means. But it did something even greater. It taught you how to believe for something that seems ridiculously impossible."

I laughed.

"Faith is a powerful tool for creation, Katharine," Don explained. "You have an unbelievable amount of it deep inside you because of those experiences. Call that faith up now. Direct it at immortality and all the topics at this conference. Faith will open it to you. You couldn't have entered this earlier. You didn't have the faith for it then. But you have the faith now."

I sighed. Was Don right? Had my life's biggest disappointments given me the building blocks for living my wildest dreams?

TRADING

"You thought those things didn't manifest because you lacked the faith or the power to make them happen," Don continued. "But that wasn't true. They didn't manifest because you traded the right to manifest those things. You laid them down for something better. You could have opened a life people dream of having. The kind of wealth, fame, and relational connections Yahweh gave you the right to possess were the things people dream of. But, deep down, you knew it would be the best of the old. It would end in death. You chose to give up the greatest things in the old for something better—a never-ending life where you build the new heaven and new earth."

"If those other things had opened, I wouldn't be sitting here now," I realized. "I'd be too absorbed with the old to venture into the new."

"You traded what can be shaken for something unshakable," Don nodded. "Look on your own timeline and tell me—do you become immortal?"

"Yes," I answered confidently. "I'm convinced of that now. I've had enough interactions with my future, immortal self. And if I become immortal, then why wouldn't I do all these other things?" I realized, my mood brightening. "And you're right that I learned a lot about faith by having faith for impossible things—even when they didn't happen. I did more than learn about faith. I grew faith inside me. I need to pull that faith out now. Sometimes, I feel like the power of my faith alone could create something out of nothing."

"Well said," Don nodded. "That's why it's important for people to take what they hear at conferences—"

"Or what they read in books," I added, grinning.

"And mix it with faith," Don finished. "Believe that it's for them. It's not just an idea they're learning about. It's not a fantasy story about the future that excites you. It's a reality for them personally. It's a description of their life. It's a personal invitation to make those things a reality in their lives."

"Not everyone who sits in these conferences or reads these books will enter in, will they?" I asked with heaviness.

"Everyone's destiny is in their own hands," Don replied. "It's like the promised land. People don't enter the new heaven and new earth because they heard it described and agreed with it. They don't enter because they have experienced a miracle or two. People enter because they walk it out to the end. They stick with it. Our job, Katharine, isn't to make sure everyone enters. Our job is to hold the door open. People will decide if they want to walk through the door or not."

Don's words were heavy. They were a potent reminder that the most critical part of a conference—or a book—is our reaction to it. Hearing powerful heavenly teaching is an open door. It's an invitation. It's what we do with it that matters.

Chapter 11

I knocked on the King of Salem's office door at our scheduled time.

"Come in," his booming voice beckoned.

His office was decorated in the same style as his library–two-story, off-white bookcases lined with colorful books filled two of the walls. Elegant chairs and coffee tables were tastefully arranged in front of floor-to-ceiling windows that took up an entire wall to the left. His desk lay on the right side, not far from a wet bar.

The king was standing at the bar when I entered, already pouring us drinks. He handed me a glass without offering for me to sit down. So I stood a foot from him, taking in his crisp features.

"What would you like to know about me, Katharine?" he asked.

"Everything."

"Well, that may take two interviews," he laughed. "Seriously, what do you not know about me that's preventing you from going deeper with me?"

"Same answer," I smiled. "It's bothering me that I don't know who you are and when you built your city or why you built it or anything about you other than that you're an impressive businessman with a fierce work ethic and a driving determination to make the universe a better place."

"Well, that's a start," he chuckled. "Do you know not everyone believes I exist? I'll be a controversial figure for a while. Some will say I'm not real. But whether you see me as a person or a being or energy or light or a thought emanating from Yahweh, it doesn't really matter. If people interact with me, they can do things that would be difficult to do otherwise. And the most powerful way to interact with me is to believe I'm real."

I smiled. "That makes sense."

"To answer your other question, I built my city a long time ago, in a different era."

"When Melchizedek lived?" I asked. "In Hebrews 11, it says that Abraham was looking forward to the city whose builder and architect was Yahweh (Heb. 11:10). I heard the city he was waiting to live in was Salem–the city you built. Is that true?"

The king chuckled. "I like that. I like thinking of the effort I made to design and build my city as effort that Yahweh himself made. Don't you?"

"I would also feel honored if I made something and others referred to it as something Yahweh did," I smiled. "It was that stunning?"

"It *is* that stunning, Katharine," Salem chuckled. "I invite you to take a look yourself. I used blueprints that are so solid Yahweh still intends to use the city as a model for many things."

"So your city was on the earth at some point? And then Yahweh removed it from this dimension to a different realm? He was keeping it hidden until it was time for the blueprints of the new heaven and new earth to be revealed?" I peppered him with questions. But before the king could answer, I continued, "That makes sense to me. Salem is part of the name Jerusalem, of course. I always thought Abraham was looking for a heavenly Jerusalem. I was even taught in seminary that the name Jerusalem is plural in Hebrew. (It has the plural ending.) Some scholars believe the plural ending was Yahweh's hint that two cities exist–one on earth and one in heaven. So I've always suspected that there was an earthly city we know from archeology and a heavenly city whose blueprints carry a level of power, glory, and splendor that the earthly city hasn't yet reflected. Is your city the one Yahweh took to a different realm? Was the fact that he removed your city from earth preserved in the name of the city itself–a name that is plural?"

"Whoa, Katharine, that's a lot of questions," Salem took half a step back. "There's a lot I could tell you about Salem. It's a beautiful, wonderful city. I still love it dearly." I could feel his heart swell as he thought about the city. "I still make that city my home–in addition to my spiritual house, of course," he winked. "There are people who built the city with me. When they saw my heart and I shared my vision with them, they gave themselves wholeheartedly to the work of building the city with me. I wish you could include each of their stories in this book, too. They deserve to be honored with me as you tell people about who I am and what I've done.

"But here's what I want to share with you now," the king continued. "Abraham was looking for a city whose blueprint didn't originate at the frequency that other cities on earth are built around–things like selfish power, control, desire to dominate. He was searching for a city that an unshakable kingdom could be built on. He knew that with a solid foundation–with the right heavenly blueprint–he could form a lasting dynasty. Anything can be built from the right foundation, can't it, Katharine?"

Salem smiled at me coyly.

"Abraham knew that Yahweh wanted to build a lasting dynasty through him? So he knew he couldn't build on the selfish, controlling foundations of other empires?" I asked.

"Yahweh had put eternity in Abraham's heart. So Abraham knew he was building for eternity," Salem answered. "That's something your generation has in common with him."

"We're building for eternity?"

"Yahweh has awakened eternity in your hearts. Yours is the first generation to demand–as a generation of people–to open the eternal aspects of life, abundance, finances, and time, among other things. You want those things opened because you want what Abraham wanted–to build an unshakable kingdom. You will establish things that can never be shaken."

"Like Salem," I whispered.

"Like my city," the king nodded.

For a long moment, I looked him in the eye. His face was young and striking, as always. Today, however, it looked like someone had buttered his skin with minuscule diamonds. He sparkled in a weirdly beautiful way.

"I see some of the principles you built Salem around," I spoke slowly, not taking my eyes from his. "Wisdom, truth, fairness, abundance. You built your city to honor those principles. Everything in your city flows through them."

Salem smiled.

"I can see why something truly built in relationship with those principles would be unshakable. And not of this world," I added. "You built in faith, not fully seeing the future. But you also built your city based on what you knew would be needed in the future. You saw this day–the day Yahweh would release the blueprints for the new heaven and new earth. And you built your city with those blueprints in mind."

"Keep going," Salem urged.

"You'll make your blueprints available to those who want to build like you did. Many others will found an unshakable kingdom by following your example."

"Excellent," Salem smiled. "That's what I wanted in the book. You're dismissed."

"Yes, sir," I replied, gathering my notes and leaving.

But when I reached the door, Salem called out to me. "One more thing, Katharine. You've been spending time with my friends Moshe and Don since you've gotten here."

I gulped. Did he know what we had done? Was I in trouble? And I had forgotten to ask Salem about the candles.

"Don't question when they tell you I wouldn't mind you doing something in my house or that I'd like you to have something," the king continued. "They speak for me while they're in my house. I know you're not used to having friends whose words carry so much authority. But you'll get used to it. They're not like your other friends whose judgment it may be wise to question at times. Trust them."

"Yes, sir," I nodded.

"You may have the candles. But don't put them in the public library. Use them yourself. You're dismissed."

Chapter 12

I decided to skip lunch so I could return to the attic. I wasn't about to open anything by myself. But the contents of that room beckoned me. When I unlocked the door and entered the room, I was in for a surprise.

"What are you doing here?" I gasped.

Don was sitting at Salem's old desk, pouring over a book with light from a Candle of Illumination. I'm unsure which startled me more—his presence or the room's appearance. Everything had been dusted and organized. Salem's desk was now clutter-free, standing in the middle of the room. The rest of the room's contents were sorted by type—books in one corner, inventions in another, treasures in a third. I stood gazing at it all with wide eyes.

"What's so surprising, Katharine?" Don asked, grinning.

"I'm puzzled about how you entered a locked room that only Salem and I have the key to," I replied.

"I may have the master key to this place," Don answered.

"You have the master key to the King of Salem's house?" I gasped. "That would explain why you gave me the keys to one attic."

"The best attic," Don countered.

"I should have known these treasures would call to you as strongly as they summoned me. What are you reading?"

He held up the book so I could see the title.

"More ancient wisdom?" I smiled.

"You know what they say, 'The future is written in the past.'"

"I don't think people say that," I laughed.

"They will," Don answered confidently. "If we want to forge the future we desire, we must understand the original building blocks. To build from anything else risks building from a flawed base. We must return to the origin, see how things were crafted, and then form our designs."

"Makes sense," I nodded. "Was it your staff or mine who organized this room?"

"I believe it was mostly Clarity's handiwork," Don answered. "She found something near the book we opened last night. Want to take a look?"

JEWELRY

He handed me a rectangular, green velvet case in which jewelry would be kept. It matched the book's cover.

"Open it," Don urged.

Looking at him apprehensively, I opened the case to reveal a large pearl necklace with matching earrings.

"Do they go with the book?" I asked.

"Probably," he shrugged. "I think they carry the frequencies in the book. But probably in a muted form."

"Probably muted?"

"Do you want it?" Don asked.

"You're offering it to me?"

"That's usually what 'do you want it' means," he teased.

"Sure," I exhaled slowly. "I want to be able to entangle with those frequencies without it nearly taking my life. Maybe this jewelry will help me do it. Thank you."

"Thank Salem—and Moshe, too," Don replied. "There were pearl cufflinks beside it inside another green velvet case. I took those," he grinned. "Why don't you sit down."

"I am sitting down."

"Why don't you sit somewhere other than on top of my desk," he directed good-naturedly.

"This isn't your desk," I pointed out. "However, this desk wants to be yours. Can you feel it? It knows how to make a king great—expand his riches and influence. It longs to work with a great king and make him greater. Not that you need the help. But the desk yearns to work for you."

Don chuckled. "Yeah, I know."

I stood up and walked to the window we had looked out the night before. Seeing the room cleaned up in daylight made it feel different enough that the terrors of the night didn't haunt me. Don joined me by the window.

"See that lake?" he asked.

"The only lake visible from this window?" I grinned.

"That's the lake that the path from the back patio leads to," Don explained. "Meet me there tonight after the evening's events. There's something important I want to show you for the book that I can only show you there."

"Sure, I'll do it with no questions asked," I replied.

"You can ask questions, Katharine."

"I'd rather have it shrouded in mystery. I like a good mystery," I explained.

Chapter 13

I opened the door to what I thought was my first afternoon lecture. I found myself in a large office with a desk and towering bookshelves. In the center of the room, a circular platform rose a foot off the ground. On it, three chairs were placed around a small, oval table. Three kings sat on those chairs.

"We summoned you here officially," the King of Righteousness spoke.

I understand that people see heavenly beings differently. How many forms has Yahweh taken in visions, for example? To me, the King of Righteousness has dark skin and golden eyes. Like the other kings, his features are flawless. His robes are costly and regal. The King of Peace appears to me to have brown skin and dark eyes. He, too, has a flawless countenance. Like most heavenly beings I've seen, all three kings look stunning and perfect.

"What do you think of the conference so far?" they asked.

"Your lecturers talk in parables," I replied, examining some books in the bookcases as I spoke. "They state things in the simplest terms. Yet deeper meaning can be mined about twenty layers down."

"That's not what we meant," the King of Peace answered. "What do you think about the people at the conference?"

I knew he meant the people on earth in this movement. I was new to all this and still getting my feet wet. "I can feel your concern for your people," I told them. You want to administer things well. And part of that is shepherding the people in this movement or tribe."

"Yes," the king nodded.

"And you want my assessment of what could be done, now that I've seen a bit of where people are firsthand," I continued. "Honestly, I think you need more teaching about who you guys are and what you're doing. It's new. It's confusing. Who you three are is so unusual that even some people leading on earth can't explain it in a sentence or two. I'm wondering if a book like this would be helpful."

Their spirits tugged on mine in an official, heavy way. Without question, they wanted me to start seriously thinking about publishing the book.

"I wasn't planning on publishing this book anytime soon," I told them. "But after seeing things, I'm thinking maybe I should. I don't know," I sighed. "I haven't been involved in the Sons of God tribe."

"We don't have a problem with that, Katharine," the King of Salem assured. Then I realized that the kings were looking for people who wanted to work with them to build the new heaven and new earth. They didn't care about what people had been doing. They only cared about what you wanted for your life from this moment forward.

I smiled. "It's not just that I haven't been involved with you guys," I gulped, my eyes scouring the floor nervously. "I've developed teachings and a small following. If I suddenly jump on board with the King of Salem and what you're doing, I'm not sure I could keep doing what I've been doing. It's not that it's at odds *per se*."

"But it's not fully compatible?" the King of Righteousness interjected.

"What if people think I'm abandoning what I've been teaching? Who will lead what I've opened if I start writing from the King of Salem's house?"

Then, a truth hit me. Three times recently, I had been given the option to leave everything else to work at the level of my highest purposes. Three times, I had said yes. Swearing to Yahweh in the realms that you'll give everything for him is one thing. Following through with that promise on earth is the difficult part.

I gulped. Now was the moment I had to decide that I'd do on earth what I had sworn to heaven I was serious about. I was at a never-go-back crossroads. If I told the kings that I would publish this book, it would set a ball in motion where I would end up laying down on earth the people and things dearest to me so I could build the new heaven and new earth with the King of Salem. I would have to die to myself on multiple levels, again and again. Did I have the guts to do it?

"It would please us if you publish this book, Katharine," the kings announced officially. "It will bring many into the truths you're beginning to unpack. Imagine helping others step into the highest purposes for their lives like you've done with yours."

"Whatever you've given up to get here, we promise to make it up to you a thousandfold," the King of Salem swore. "Working with us is never second best."

"I have no doubt," I smiled weakly. "It just costs someone everything."

"The best things do," he answered.

"I love the life I've built for myself. I thought it was everything I ever wanted. But when I look at you, Salem," I told the king, holding his gaze, "I feel your worth so deeply that I don't want to be anywhere else, doing anything else. Everything else tastes horrible compared to what's flowing from you—and the people around you."

The king smiled warmly, amusement dancing on the corners of his lips. He opened his mouth slightly like he was going to speak. But then he changed his mind. Although his lips didn't move, I heard his voice in my head, saying, "I swear to you, Katharine, that you won't be disappointed. No one ever is."

"Why do I find myself dumping all that I am and all I've accomplished at your feet—again and again?" I answered him out loud.

"Because you're not stupid," he replied. A smile played on his lips. But I knew he wasn't really joking.

"There's nothing else I want to be doing," I announced my decision quietly, my head bowed.

I felt like my words were being recorded into an official record even though I didn't notice a scribe. Something had just shifted in heaven and earth for my life. Tears, unbidden, streamed down my cheeks. Giving up everything for something greater is a reason to celebrate. But it's also a reason to mourn. The loss of things dear to you is real.

Moved, the king stepped down to stand in front of me. "You're going to come through this," he promised, his eyes full of compassion, "with far more than you brought into our agreement." His eyes searched mine for several moments until he assured himself I would be okay emotionally. "You're dismissed, Katharine. But we're never really apart, are we?"

In his voice, I could hear concern for me—fused with amusement that I was so emotional about the transition. He knew it would have a happy ending. How could it not? I was going to be working with him.

Chapter 14

Closing the door to the kings' conference room slowly, I inched down the hall. I was deep in thought. When someone sprinting by bumped into me, it jarred me back to the present. Realizing I was officially late, I began racing down the hall myself. I didn't want to miss the afternoon lecture.

When I swung the door open to what I thought was the correct conference room, I found myself in a lounge full of people. Melchizedek was directly in front of me. The King of Salem was there, too, standing to my right. Solomon, Moshe, and one of Don's friends on earth scurried around the room. The angel Metatron was seated in a chair near the doorway. When he saw me, he rose. The keys dangling from his belt sounded at a deafening frequency. No one else seemed bothered by it.

"Katharine, welcome. You're late. Come sit by me," he said.

Hugging me with one arm, he gestured to the chair next to him. But before I could be seated, the being Life approached.

"I need to speak to her first," she informed the angel.

"Thank you, but I'm trying to get to a lecture," I told them both.

"You're in the best seat for the lecture," Melchizedek smiled. "You're in what we call the waiting room. This room is where it's determined what will be released through the talk the person gives. You can influence things from here. We're assessing the audience. We're also assessing the entire earth—what earth is ready for now and in the next few years. We'll formulate a plan here. The lecturer can decide what to release from what's in this room. If there's no place to land something now, it stays here. That's why we call this the waiting room. It will wait here until it can be released publicly. But you can benefit from the teaching here, whether or not it gets released to the public today," he winked.

"I think I follow all that," I nodded. "So who's the speaker?"

"Don's speaking next," Don's friend on earth informed everyone. I'll call the friend Timotheus for the purposes of the book.

"I thought his talk was later today."

"It got bumped up," Melchizedek answered. "Things need to be rearranged sometimes."

"We're reviewing some documents to see if we should okay them for release," Timotheus announced. Looking at me, he asked, "Want to join us?"

I glanced at Life. "In a second," I told him.

Life whispered as she pulled me aside, her hand resting on my arm. "Sorry to do this here and now."

When I looked her in the eyes, the room disappeared. She had transported us to a different realm.

LIFE

"You're in a realm centered on life," she began. "You wonder what life is. Taste me and find out."

"I usually taste a flow spilling from someone's feet," I told her. "I don't see a flow coming from you. How do you want me to taste you? Take a bite out of your arm?"

"If you wish," she answered. I couldn't tell if she was joking.

I leaned over her. To my surprise, I was a couple of inches taller. When my head came close to her form, pictures flashed through my mind. I saw people doing all sorts of things—living life. The closer I got to her, the faster the images flashed.

"I'm sorry, but I can't take a bite from your perfect arm," I announced.

So I breathed her in. "You are power mixed with joy and purpose and direction. You always give. You're never-ending. In your deepest places, you hold wisdom and might. Every good thing can be found in you. When someone holds you fully, they possess everything that Bible verse talks about. What is it? 'Whatever is true, whatever is honorable, whatever is just, whatever is pure, whatever is lovely, whatever is commendable, if there is any excellence, if there is anything worthy of praise' (Phil. 4:8 ESV). That is what you are. That's a very crude beginning to explaining you."

"It's not so crude," Life replied, honored. "That's who you are. I am a partial reflection of you. I was created as a being to remind you of what this aspect of your nature is. If you forget, if you want to gaze at your beauty only as it's reflected in me, then you can interact with me."

"Well said," I smiled. "Show me around."

"I am held in the deepest places of every individual," Life spoke as she approached the edge of a pool. "The only thing more powerful than me is you. If you choose not to believe in me, recognize me, or hold onto me, I remain buried inside you. People must awaken to me and pull me up. When they do, nothing can stop me from flowing in you and through you to all of creation."

"I can feel your power when you say that," I told her. "You are an unstoppable power. Far stronger than death."

"Death cannot touch me," Life announced.

"Then why do people die?"

"Because they choose to keep me locked up, imprisoned with a fraction of my power. They believe lies that tell them they deserve death or that life will end for them," she answered. "You don't believe those lies."

"Not anymore," I nodded. "My soul and my body—"

"Are perfect," Life cut in. "Please don't tell people they need to fix their souls and bodies before they can interact with me. Come to me as you are. Embrace me in your pain, in your confusion, in your suffering. That's what you did."

"I took a lot of approaches," I winked. "That was one of them."

"And it worked."

"I bet a lot of approaches would work," I answered. "The goal is to have all of us—body, soul, and spirit—experience that perfection. I asked you to show me the way to never-ending life. I thought you'd share wisdom or have something for me to do. But you didn't start with that. You started at the foundation. You showed me there was no reason that I shouldn't live. Life accepted me. I wasn't judged or condemned for anything I had done. I was innocent and pure."

"That's right," Life beamed. "But there's more."

"When I wanted intimacy with Yahweh," I backed up to explain, "I wanted to jump straight to mind-blowing encounters. But that's not where he started. He started by laying a new foundation of love in my life. He spent weeks—maybe months—making me feel completely loved by him. From that foundation, we could build the type of intimacy I wanted. You took the same approach. I asked for never-ending life. You started by laying a new foundation of life inside me. When we realize that every part of us is acceptable in every part of creation, there's no reason we shouldn't live forever. I know that sounds simple, but that's why people die. We believe we deserve death. We feel condemned. We don't feel worthy for every part of us to stand in every part of creation.

"I had even memorized Bible verses that I believed told me I deserved death, that there was something fundamentally wrong with me, that I was a sinner and ought to die," I continued. "The part of me that still believed that kept arguing with you," I told Life. "I kept insisting there was something unacceptable about me. Why couldn't you see it? Finally, I wondered if the voice inside me telling me I was unacceptable was mistaken. The voice seemed so certain. The feeling was so ingrained. But I was persistent. I kept presenting that feeling to Life and every part of creation. Eventually, I realized the message written inside me wasn't that I was an unacceptable sinner. It was that I was perfect. That was my original frequency, the original message. My reading of that frequency had gotten twisted. I thought it was singing, 'You're unworthy. There's something wrong with you.' But really, it was singing, 'You're worthy. You're like God.' Somehow, it distorted, so I heard one message although the original one was completely different. Maybe that happened at the Fall. I don't know. I'm just glad I figured out what the original message was."

Life smiled broadly.

"Then my soul felt as worthy and capable as my spirit," I continued. "I felt worthy of Life. So I could fully embrace you—a reflection of me."

"Beautiful," Life smiled. "Take a look around here. It's all yours. Take whatever you need. Then hurry back to the conference."

LEGAL SYSTEM

"One more thing," I called as she turned to leave. "The Bible talks about the 'law of sin and death' versus the 'law of life' (Rom. 8:2). When we believe that we're worthy of life, when we feel completely worthy, then we've moved from the 'law of sin and death' into the 'law of life.' We are divine beings. We decide what law we'll put ourselves under. Humanity has enslaved ourselves to sin and death. Yahweh gave us the Law. He gave us the Cross. They pull us out of death and into life. But we haven't taken what the Law and the Cross do for us and applied it so we feel forgiven and acceptable—all the way to our core. When we feel acceptable and worthy, though, we switch the set of rules that govern our lives. Death cannot come for us. Life is the law that is enforced in us."

"Well said, Katharine," Life answered. "There's more. But that's good for now."

LAKE

I decided to jump into the lake in the realm of Life. Feet first, I plunged in. There, I found the Apostle John, staring at me, all smiles. He had unlocked Life's mysteries. Without words, he called, "Dive into the deeper mystery with me."

So I swam up to him. With my hair wildly floating around me, I hovered in front of John so we could chat. I knew he had something important to say for the book. And I knew the first thing out of his mouth would be spoken to every person reading the book.

He said, "The reason you're on earth is more important than you think."

Instantly, something inside me unlocked. "You understood the mysteries of Life and Light," I told him. "Teach them to us now."

"I unpacked those mysteries through my close relationship with Yeshua," John answered. "To understand what I did, examine my connection to him. Read the Bible passages about Yeshua and me again, pondering our connection. That was my path. I open it to you."

"Thanks," I replied. "But most people can't do that. We can't read the Bible and peer deeply into what you and Yeshua were doing that wasn't recorded in the scriptures. It's harder than you think to use the Bible as a portal into the actual events. Can you just tell us?"

"Alright," he agreed. "But you'll glean more if you look at it yourself, too. I came to realize Yeshua's deep love for me. That love unlocked places in my heart that allowed me to overcome trauma. I moved beyond the troubles of this world. I focused on my heavenly estate. From that estate, many mysteries opened to me. Start there."

"Thank you," I grinned.

I stayed with John for a while, breathing with him to take my understanding of what he was saying deeper inside me. After soaking in the pool for a long time, I emerged, dripping from head to toe. Small beings of light were waiting for me on the shore.

"We're emissaries of light," they called. "We're here to do your bidding.

We're released to those who dip in the pool and remember who they are."

"And the powers housed inside them," another miniature being added.

"Come with me," I directed. "We're going somewhere together."

AWAKE

I stepped back into the waiting room. Four or five of the light beings floated around me. Some were looking at the others there in wonder. Some seemed bored. They wanted to be given something to do.

"She's awake," Salem announced. "Katharine has woken up."

Had I been asleep on a sofa here while interacting with Life? Or was he speaking in a parable? Had I been asleep, dying, and now I was waking up to life and who I really am?

"Katharine's awake!" Melchizedek confirmed, excited.

Moshe and Metatron rushed over. Half the room was hovering over me as I stirred. I wanted to get to work right away. "Let's start unpacking Life," I told them eagerly. "I want to bring never-ending life and ever-increasing beauty to the earth. I want the people on earth to look and feel as stunningly beautiful as the people in heaven. I believe that's how we were supposed to be."

Metatron and Melchizedek were the first to speak. "We want you to begin knowing you'll succeed," they announced.

"And it won't take you as long as you think," Melchizedek added. "Momentum is swinging in that direction already."

I sat up fully, patting one of the light beings beside me. I was about to open my mouth when something registered inside me.

"Don's taken the microphone," Timotheus announced, hushing every other conversation in the room. He was peeking through the barely-opened door to the adjacent conference room.

"Positions, everyone!" Melchizedek ordered. "It's game time."

Melchizedek wasn't kidding about positions. Timotheus stayed by the door. He whispered loudly occasionally, informing us about the audience's reaction. He also updated us about what the angels in the room were doing, which people from the cloud of witnesses showed up, what portals were opening, and the like.

Melchizedek paced, refusing to sit down. He seemed deep in thought the entire time. Metatron and the King of Salem sat in white, plush chairs next to each other. I happened to sit right across from them. Metatron was listening carefully to Don's every word. Salem, on the other hand, was smiling at me.

"Do you want to know what we're opening here, Katharine?" he asked, grinning. "It's a new era. Nothing will be the same after this. Mark my words."

I nodded respectfully. I was straining to hear Don's words in the other room while taking in everything happening in this room.

"Some people will minimize what happens here and what we're doing," Salem continued. He seemed oblivious to my efforts to listen to the lecture. "I'll still work with some people who ignore me or deny my existence. So will you. But the ones who acknowledge who I am and seek to work with me will flow better with me. Therefore, they will do more, go farther."

"Won't how much they do depend on many factors, Salem—not just if they're aware of who you are and what's going on here?" I answered.

"True, but my point remains, too, Katharine. Don't forget it." He rose to sit in the chair next to me. For a long moment, he looked me in the eyes intently. His gaze stirred something deep inside me. "I want to start working with you," he declared.

"What's holding you back?" I asked, laughing for half a second.

Holding my gaze steadily, he said, "Our partnership will continue for decades. Mark my words." Then he rose to return to his original seat.

Chapter 15

In the adjacent room, Don had begun his lecture. "This isn't just a conference. It's a gathering of the Sons of Lights for what we are moving forward into. I need to speak to you about one of the most important things—perhaps the most important thing—we can move into at this time."

I could feel the room leaning forward, sitting on the edge of their seats. In the waiting room, I also inched forward on my elegant chair.

Don continued, "The Bible says, 'For every one that useth milk is unskilful in the word of righteousness: for he is a babe. But strong meat belongeth to them that are of full age, even those who by reason of use have their senses exercised to discern both good and evil. Therefore leaving the principles of the doctrine of Christ, let us go on unto perfection' (Heb. 5:13–6:1 KJV).

"Our quest is to move away from the yummy Papa God milk—the feel-good doctrines of infancy. We're heading into perfection," Don explained.

In the waiting room, the King of Salem raised his eyebrows at me, making sure I heard that point. "This is about perfection, Katharine," he whispered.

PERFECTION

"Think about what Paul says," Don continued. "'Forgetting those things which are behind, and reaching forth unto those things which are before, I press toward the goal for the prize of the upward call of God in Christ Jesus' (Phil. 3:13–14 KJV). "What was the prize Paul was straining to reach?"

"Perfection?" I guessed to myself, waiting to hear Don's answer.

"Paul came to me and quoted those verses that he wrote. Then he explained what he was going after," Don told the crowd, animated. "The prize—the supernatural inheritance—God has reserved for us is perfection. And beyond perfection lies the crown of sovereignty. Only those who are deemed perfect will be entrusted with it. If you want to be equal to and the spitting image of the one who gave you life, you need to be perfect."

I realized Don was talking about Matthew 5:48, where Yeshua said, "Be perfect, therefore, as your heavenly Father is perfect" (NIV). Yeshua wouldn't have told us to be perfect unless it was completely possible—and extremely important—to be perfect.

"Peter also says that we 'may become partakers of the divine nature, having escaped from the corruption that is in the world because of sinful desire,'" Don continued (2 Pet. 1:4 ESV). "This is the day and hour where we can do what Paul, Yeshua, and Peter spoke about. We're getting the technology and the tools to taste perfection and then to walk into what perfection looks like."

In the waiting room, Salem was smiling at me broadly. With his eyes, he urged me to soak in every detail of Don's message. I knew people had tried for millennia to be perfect. Many tried by good works to reach perfection. But that path led only to death. The wisest among us realized that we were created in the perfect image of God. Perfection already resides inside us. So they tried—through the Law or the Cross—to agree with what Yahweh had already spoken about us. When Yahweh breathed himself into Adam, he testified about who we are. Yahweh's breath, living in us, is meant to speak to us continually that we are like him. Don was calling us to agree with Yahweh's testimony about us. We do bear his image. We are perfect. Yahweh says so. Every other voice is false.

SOVEREIGNTY

"Beyond perfection lies the crown of sovereignty," Don continued. "Only those who are perfect will be entrusted with it. What is sovereignty? Sovereignty isn't just moving in divine power. The full face of sovereignty will be when we look like one who is equal to Yahweh."

When Don spoke those words, many in the audience gasped in astonishment. Some coughed as their old mindsets came up to be either spewed out or swallowed back down.

"If it's hard to fully agree with what I just said," Don responded, "I hope you can treat the matter as Jacob did. When Joseph had a dream that was difficult to accept, Jacob rebuked him. But the Bible also says he kept the matter in his heart. If you need to rebuke something—if the people you lead on earth rebuke this teaching—that's okay. Rebuke if you have to. But also keep the matter in your heart. Because the same God we all serve will eventually lead us into all truth."

I could feel people's smiles in reaction to Don's words. He had given them permission to disagree with anything he said. But he had encouraged them not to push a teaching away simply because they disagreed with it. Let the idea filter through you. Let it rest in your heart. Then your heart, which you share with God, will lead you in the way you should go.

FRAMEWORK

"Let me back up and give you a way to understand this journey," Don continued. "The Bible says to present yourself as a living sacrifice to God (Rom. 12:1). When you do that, the scroll—the mission or purpose for your life—is taken from inside you and presented to you. But the scroll is sealed. Do you remember how many seals were on the scroll in Revelation 5?"

"Seven," a few people in the audience shouted.

"Right. Your life scroll is also sealed with seven seals. Those seals are related to the seven spirits of God," Don explained.

Don referred to Isaiah 11:2-3: "And the spirit of the LORD shall rest upon him, the spirit of wisdom and understanding, the spirit of counsel and might, the spirit of knowledge and of the fear of the LORD" (KJV). If you count them, seven spirits—seven expressions of God's nature—are listed in those verses.

"When you present your scroll to Yahweh, those seven seals get loosed," Don continued. "The seven spirits begin to tutor you to maturity so you can fulfill what's written on your scroll. Once you mature, the seven spirits go to Yahweh and say, 'We're done. This person is ready. We'll continue walking with them. But you can have them now.

"Originally, you presented your scroll—the book of your life—to Yahweh. When you're mature and ready to begin doing what's written in that book, Yahweh presents your book to creation. Once that happens, you can begin the journey to perfection and then sovereignty."

MATURITY

"Do you know what maturity looks like?" Don asked, his eyes full of wonder. "Ask Paul. Paul says, 'Though I have the gift of prophecy, and understand all mysteries, and all knowledge; and though I have all faith, so that I could remove mountains' (1 Cor. 13:2 KJV). We tend to focus on the last part of that verse, where he says that without love, none of it functions. But do you know what he's also saying? He understood all mysteries. He possessed all knowledge. He had faith so that he could remove mountains. That is what maturity looks like.

"Paul isn't the only one who can understand all mysteries. He's not the only one who will possess all knowledge or have faith that moves mountains. Paul wrote those words in the Bible so that we will do what he did. Anyone can go on this journey. Anyone can reach the finish line.

"The Bible says God has enabled us to share in the inheritance of the saints in light (Col. 1:12). People speculate about what that inheritance is. I'll tell you what it is. It's to be like Yahweh. We will look and function just like our Father.

"Yeshua said to let your light shine so that people can see your good works and glorify your Father who is in heaven," Don continued. "What are our good works? It's not signs and wonders. It's to do precisely what Yahweh did in the beginning. Those were the good works Yahweh did. What works did Yahweh himself call his good works? Creation. He created everything and called it good. Those were his good works.

"That's what we're meant to do, too," Don spoke emphatically. "We're to become like him so that when people see us, they see his face. We've started to look and function just like him."

WAY OF LIFE

"How do we move into maturity? How do we move from maturity to perfection, then onto sovereignty?" Don asked the audience. "There are many paths. I want to tell you about one path—the Way of Life. It will lead you into sovereignty. I'll speak about it in my next lecture."

Smiling, Don left the podium and went straight to the waiting room. There were many lined up to thank him.

"Some things I've wanted to be released for a long time were released today," Melchizedek reported, smiling. "Thank you. Well done." Turning to everyone in the room, he spoke loudly, "We'll meet here tomorrow before Don's next talk. He has some important things to say about Life. We'll all do our part for that talk, too."

I glanced at Life, waiting in the corner. She was beaming broadly. I could feel the close connection she had with Don. Eventually, I made my way over to speak to Don, too. "That was important stuff," I smiled. "I'm putting every word in the book I'm writing."

"Every single word?" Don laughed. "How many pages are in your book?"

"Enough. Or are you suggesting that if I tried to write down everything you said, the whole world couldn't contain the books that could be written?" I joked, referencing what John said about Yeshua in John 21:25.

"Someday," Don winked. "But we'll start small."

"I'm afraid that's not possible. You've already started. And that was not small," I grinned. "I have some follow-up questions about your talk. Would you have time to chat at some point?"

"I have time now," Don answered. "Let me grab a snack. Meet me at the entrance to Salem's garden in ten minutes."

Chapter 16

I admit it. One of the best parts of Salem's event was the food. On the way out, I walked past table after table, where snacks of all varieties were available. Grabbing a couple of treats from other galaxies, I hurried to meet Don.

He was already at the garden entrance. I laughed when I saw him holding a king-sized picnic basket with a bottle of wine tucked into its side.

"I feel like I need to say this for the record," I told him as I drew close. "Both of us drink only occasionally on earth. When people notice the number of chapters mentioning alcohol, I don't want them to get the wrong impression."

"I think people understand the symbolism of wine in this book," Don replied, grinning. "Come on, Katharine. I've arranged a surprise and am eager to show it to you."

As we began strolling in Salem's garden, I took a moment to look around. The bright sun perfectly highlighted the exotic, beautiful flowers on display.

"I heard his most sacred flowers are kept indoors under lock and key," Don noted as we passed rare varieties few had ever seen.

"Doesn't surprise me that he'd have flowers that valuable," I replied, impressed.

There was a path that wound slowly through the expansive garden. We followed it, too much in a hurry to give the flowers a proper viewing.

"I wanted to dig deeper into your teaching," I began. "I loved the framework you gave for our spiritual journey. We start with becoming mature. From maturity, we unlock perfection. From perfection, we unlock sovereignty. Until your lecture, every teaching I heard was aimed only at the first step—bringing us to maturity. I thought maturity was the end goal. But it's actually the starting gate."

Don chuckled. "I like how you put it."

"In karate, I used to think that earning a black belt was the highest level of achievement. I had friends who worked for years to earn different color belts. When they reached black belt, I thought they were done. Then I learned that receiving a black belt meant the masters thought you were ready to begin the real instruction," I laughed. "Is that what spiritual maturity is—earning a black belt?"

"I guess you could look at it that way," Don mused.

"So a real gem in your teaching is that we can move beyond maturity to perfection. I want to know more about that. How do we reach a state of perfection?"

"The key is the soul," Don replied.

As he spoke, we rounded a curve in the path. A man wearing thick, kingly robes stood on the other side of the curve. A crown rested on his head.

"David?" I gasped. "You're here?"

"Good to see you, Katharine," he answered. After kissing my cheek in greeting, he turned to Don. "Don, a pleasure as always."

"Was he your surprise?" I asked Don.

"There's more," Don winked.

David fell in step with us, flowing with our conversation naturally. "We're talking about perfecting the soul, David," I announced. "We'd love to hear your insights."

Before David could say anything, we were drawn to a figure sitting by a small pond about twenty yards away. He was also wearing thick, kingly robes. His clothing had wrapped around his presence for so long that it was charged with some of his power. Even at this distance, I could hear his garments crackling like an electrical current was flowing through them.

"Yahweh," I said slowly and reverently.

"Come. Join me in a picnic," he called in a friendly voice. He was seated on the far side of a large picnic blanket.

"I brought the meat and the wine," Don announced, holding up the picnic basket as we approached.

"I've also brought some food of my own," Yahweh replied. "It will be a feast set for kings—and queens," he added, winking at the queen.

THE SOUL

As we settled on the blanket, David announced, "I'm opening some of my house to you and the readers, Katharine."

Suddenly, a different realm was visible behind David. Part of his house—literally—was present in our discussion. In fact, I wasn't sure if we were in Salem's garden, David's garden, or both.

David sat to Yahweh's right. Don sat to his left. I settled in between the two of them. It felt like we were about to have an important discussion that could help people awaken their souls to their perfected state.

"Many people don't understand what the soul is or its importance," Yahweh chose the first topic to dive into.

"How would you define the soul, Katharine?" David asked.

"I'm going to defer to Don for the official definition," I replied. "But, in my experience, our spirits already seem perfected. They don't carry the traumas or troubles of our lives on earth. For the people born on earth now, the soul and the body do carry a record of trauma in them. I believe a generation is coming that will be born with no trauma. And they will never have to experience trauma. But currently, people are born with trauma already in their DNA and energetic record. Perfecting the soul is about removing the record of trauma—or at least overcoming it.

"Psychologists define trauma as the record of an experience that was beyond what our level of joy was at the time the event happened," I continued. "So, it's not an event itself that causes trauma. It's how we processed the event. For example, a kid may have their bicycle stolen. If the child is really happy in other areas of their life, then their joy level exceeds the emotions of having a bike stolen. So, it doesn't create a record of trauma in the soul. However, if the child was in a lower emotional state, then having a bike stolen could be a traumatic event. The record of trauma doesn't imprint on the spirit. It's stored in the soul. That's why we're talking about bringing our souls to a perfected state.

"Sometimes people ask me how they can tell if they're interacting with their spirit or their soul," I continued. "I tell them—feelings of hopelessness or insecurity, a nagging voice that tells you things aren't going to work out or that you're worth less—those are the soul telling you what issues or traumas are imprinted on it. The soul will keep telling you the issues until they're resolved. The spirit never feels hopeless, depressed, or insecure. So if you feel the emotions of trauma present, then it's your soul you're interfacing with."

Glancing from Don and David, I added, "You'd probably remind us that in Psalm 42:5, David says, 'Why are you cast down, O my soul? Why are you disquieted within me?' (NKJV) David knows his soul feels down and upset, not his spirit. So he works with his soul to remove its record of trauma."

I glanced at Don to take it from there. "When your body was formed in the natural world, you, as a spirit being, birthed your soul as an interface between your spirit and your body. So you created your soul. You created it in your image—the perfect, divine image that your spirit bears, the image of Yahweh. Anything that you have given birth to, you are Lord over. So, it's your responsibility to be the Lord over your soul and to bring it into the reality of where you are. Our goal is to govern our soul by embracing and loving it. We want our soul to respond to who we are as a spirit being, as a Lord, as a sovereign one walking out the image of Yahweh.

"The soul is tremendously important," Don emphasized. "What you'll look like in Yahweh's world depends on what you do with your soul."

That made sense to me. The soul was created to help us function in creation, which Yahweh's world is part of. Everyone's spirit perfectly reflects the image of God. So who we are in Yahweh's world depends more on how our soul is doing than our spirit. That's why soul work is so important.

PERFECTING THE SOUL

"Don, why don't you share what David showed you about how he worked with his soul," Yahweh suggested.

"Sure," Don nodded. "David showed me a three-step process he did with his soul. He asked his soul, 'What can I do to love you into perfection?' And then he did things to help the soul feel his love so it could realize its own perfection."

"That's beautiful," I interjected.

"I watched David as he was in his courtyard during his life on earth," Don began. "I saw him standing there. Opposite him, something was standing there that looked like a mirror reflection of him. But it was translucent. David was breathing into it. He was allowing his breath to wrap itself around what was staring at him face to face. It was as if a whole whirlwind of his breath enveloped what was standing before him."

I glanced over at David. He was smiling.

Don continued, "Then he took it to places spiritually—his personal garden, his places of war, chambers of Yahweh. Eventually, I realized what was staring at David was his soul."

"I loved my soul," David spoke up. "It was a gradual process for me—

awakening to realize how deeply I loved my soul. But when my love fully stirred, it was fierce. I don't think there's anything I wouldn't do for it."

"Our spirit loves our soul deeply," I agreed. "But our soul awakens to realize that love—as we may awaken to perceiving how fervently Yeshua always loved us. The first time my soul experienced it, she noticed a spiritual being standing in front of her. Then she realized the being was my spirit. My spirit being bent down, looked my soul in the eyes, and said, 'I love you.' Instantly, my soul was hit with an overpowering sense of being loved—not by God, but by myself, by my own spirit. That sparked a journey of my soul awakening to who she is."

"I let Don see how much I loved my soul and what I did to help it," David nodded. "Later, I showed him where I wrote about it in the Bible—Psalm 42."

"David showed me three main things he did to love his soul to perfection," Don explained. "They are linked to where he says, 'Why are you cast down, O my soul?' (Ps. 42:5,11).

"So, when his soul started to tell him how bad it was feeling, he didn't ignore it? He asked it why it was feeling bad?" I asked.

"Right. He didn't shove the bad feelings away. He spoke to his soul lovingly," Don nodded. "After asking his soul why it was feeling down, he enveloped it in his breath—the record of who he is as a spirit being. Then he took his soul, while wrapped in his breath, to look at the face of Yahweh and remember who Yahweh is."

"Wow," I looked from David to Don and back again. "So when you had 'soul emotions' like discouragement, you wrapped your soul in your breath and took him to look at Yahweh?"

"You've done something similar, Katharine," David answered.

"I never thought to wrap my soul in my breath. But I have enabled her to have her own encounters with Yahweh. Sometimes, the soul will watch our spiritual encounters but not feel part of them because she feels unworthy or disqualified. She can hear Yahweh say, 'I love you,' and think he's talking to my spirit, not her. So I think it's brilliant that you took your soul to have its own face-to-face time with Yahweh."

"Right. David wrapped his soul in his breath, then said, 'Look at Yahweh. Look at his exploits. Remember his countenance. Hope in God,'" Don explained. "What is Yahweh's countenance? It's his Faces. It's the display of the glory that radiates from his face when we look at him."

NEXT STEP

"Then David turned his spirit to Yahweh, and he breathed face-to-face with Yahweh," Don continued. "I've taught people the method I saw David using as he breathed with Yahweh."

"Wow," I smiled. "What does breathing face-to-face with Yahweh do?"

"It gets you flowing in total sync with him," Don answered. "So it gives your soul another divine countenance to look at and be transformed by. Perfecting your soul isn't Yahweh's responsibility. It's yours. Sometimes, I do things in my life simply to show my soul that there is a greater reality behind who I am. I want it to see my goodness as a sovereign one and conform to my image."

"That's the perspective of maturity," I realized. "So first, you show your soul who Yahweh is. Then, you breathe with Yahweh to get fully in sync with him. And you say to your soul, 'Look at my goodness. Look at the purity of my heart. Look at where I am.' So the soul needs to see both Yahweh and you—its creator—to reach perfection faster?"

"Having your spirit and Yahweh arcing over your soul makes the experience much more powerful for your soul," Don explained.

"So what do you do as you're arcing over your soul?" I asked.

"Let me show you what David did. Going back to Psalm 42, David says, 'I will remember you from the land of the Jordan, the heights of Hermon—from Mount Mizar' (Ps. 42:6). Those are the places of David's encounters with Yahweh. They're the places of his victories in war.

They're the places of his intimacy. David brings those things to mind."

"He says he's remembering from those places. So did he relive—in this mind at least—all the victories Yahweh had given him? All the special moments they shared?" I asked.

"Yes, absolutely," Don nodded. "It was an active remembering. A stepping-back-into-it kind of thing."

"He made those past experiences feel real to him again," I replied. I glanced at David to see if he had anything to add. He was silent.

LAST STEP

"Finally, David turned back to his soul, letting the billows and waves of Yahweh crash over it. He writes, 'Deep calls to deep in the roar of your waterfalls; all your waves and breakers have swept over me'" (Ps. 42:7 NIV). Which waterfall is he talking about?" Don asked rhetorically. "What's flowing is a stream that comes from Yahweh's house into his personal garden because it's his personal place of intimacy with Yahweh."

"That's profound," I interjected. "Waterfalls do represent an intimate, forceful stream from Yahweh. The flow will hit you much harder while standing under a waterfall than when wading in a brook. And since David says, 'Deep calls to deep,' he's talking about sharing your depths with each other."

"Right," Don nodded. "David is in his garden now, spiritually. He's in the place of intimacy. The place where he's planted and cultivated the roses and bouquets of his intimacy with Yahweh."

Slowly, I looked around. Is that why Don wanted to meet in the garden? We were in the kind of place David went spiritually when he wanted to love his soul to perfection. When I glanced at David, he was grinning.

"The waves are the sound and the refreshment of his soul. They crash over him from his personal space with Yahweh in his garden," Don explained.

"For me, during intimate encounters with Yahweh, it feels like waves are hitting my entire being. The frequency of those waves is so insanely high that they can wipe away the darkest soul emotions in seconds. Often, I've taken my soul into those waves on purpose. I've used their frequency to erase trauma from the soul."

"I've seen Katharine do that," David said.

"I've witnessed you doing that, too," I laughed. "And you wrote about it in the Bible."

"I wrote a song about it. And I sang it over my soul in some of my darkest moments," David replied. "'By day the LORD directs his love, at night his song is with me,'" he said softly, quoting Psalm 42:8 (NIV). "The waves and breakers are the love of Yahweh—his deep, passionate love which I felt and shared with my soul."

"That's what Don's saying. He's saying you're letting the waves pour over your soul in your garden—your intimate place," I replied. "Most people miss that point. But I think it's an important key. If we try to refresh our soul outside of the garden and its intimacy, the waves lose much of their power."

"To summarize," Don cleared his throat, "David enveloped his soul in his breath and took it to look at Yahweh face to face. Then David's spirit turned his attention to Yahweh and exchanged breath with him, remembering who Yahweh is and all he's done for him. That formed an arc between his spirit and Yahweh over his soul so his soul could look at Yahweh's image in Yahweh *and* in David's spirit. Finally, David turned his attention back to his soul, allowing the waves and billows of deep intimacy to wash over his soul."

PICNIC

"Wonderful," Yahweh proclaimed. "Let's eat."

While the rest of us had been caught up in our conversation, Yahweh had spread the food in the center of the blanket. Happily, we dug into a kingly feast. As we talked and laughed, Yahweh asked us questions about what Don had just unpacked.

"What was the most important part of the process for you, David?" Yahweh queried.

"Loving my soul. You can walk through all the steps. But if you do them with love for your soul, you will get so much more from it," David answered. "Love transforms."

"Katharine?" Yahweh asked next.

"'All your waves and breakers have swept over me' (Ps. 42:7 NIV)—that's the most powerful part for me. I've brought my soul and body into those waves and breakers—sometimes for hours. It's the most effective tool I've used to clear trauma from the soul," I answered. "The second most effective tool I've used is encouraging my soul to have her own encounters with Yahweh. So, I think how Don and David put it together in a three-step process is unbelievably powerful. But can I say something else?"

"Of course," Yahweh replied.

"Like Don, I've taught people how to do some of these things David did with his soul. I've found that few people can hear an explanation and—from that alone—reproduce it in their lives. So, I've developed exercises and activations. With those tools, most people can experience these things powerfully."

"Perhaps we should create some material that would help people love their souls to perfection as David did," Don mused aloud.

"Perhaps we should. We could tell people to check the website to see what materials are available," I replied.

"Develop whatever tools you want to give people," Yahweh replied. "I see your hearts intend to help people in the greatest way possible."

Then Yahweh opened the wine he had brought, and the fun really began. At first, I intended to spend an hour or so in the garden and then return to the conference. But I was having too much fun to leave.

Eventually, Don and I decided to skip the afternoon sessions and hang out with Yahweh and David in Salem's garden. How many times do you get the chance to do that?

DAVID'S GARDEN

Later in the afternoon, while Yahweh and Don were deep in conversation, David said to me, "I want to show you my garden. Come with me."

So we stepped out of Salem's place and into David's garden in his spiritual spaces. Flowers and plants of all varieties lined the clearing before us. For several minutes, David showed me one after another, explaining their significance.

"Remember my Mighty Men?" David asked.

"The warriors mentioned in 2 Samuel 23?" I asked.

"They gave me this bouquet," David pointed to a cluster of roses. "Smell it."

Each flower in the garden released a fragrance associated with the person or event it commemorated. When I inhaled the roses from the Mighty Men, I exclaimed, "Oh wow! I think I know what it's like to get a testosterone injection. There is some powerful masculine energy on that!"

David laughed loudly. "Look at my pool over here, Katharine," he called. "Bend down and peer into it."

The water showed me a reflection of myself—in full queenly attire. Quickly, I double-checked what I was actually wearing. I still had my regular outfit on.

"You wonder why you look like a queen when you peer into my pool?" David asked, grinning. "That pool holds a reflection of who I am. You're looking inside me, sensing one of my attributes, and then it's causing the same thing that rests inside you to come to the surface. So, as you look into me, you come to reflect the part of me you look at. You're used to doing that by looking into someone's eyes or going into their depths. You can do it with a pool, too."

"Fascinating," I replied. "Show me your waterfall—the one you talk about in Psalm 42."

"Maybe some other time," David replied.

"But I'd love to taste the love you and Yahweh developed. Everyone's relationship with Yahweh forms its own flavor of divine love. I'd love to taste yours," I explained.

"If you want to taste my unique walk with Yahweh, drink my wine," David suggested. Instantly, he held a goblet of it and offered it to me. "This has the record of what you seek inside it."

Looking David in the eye, I held his cup to my lips and drank deeply. Without warning, we were in the Cave of Adullam, where he hid from Saul. The David who lived on earth was leaning against a cave wall, afraid and discouraged. The David I had been interacting with stood beside me. Then I witnessed what the scared, discouraged David did with those emotions. He realized it was his soul who felt frightened and dismayed. He wanted to use his circumstance to teach his soul who it was.

"You partnered with your darkest moments, seeing them as opportunities to mature your soul?" I whispered to the David next to me.

"The darkest moments of life are some of the best times to clear the soul of its troubles. I saw them as fantastic opportunities—not something that must be endured or gotten through as quickly as possible," he answered. "That's what I wanted to show you."

Suddenly, we were back in his garden. The goblet of his wine was still in my hands. "Keep drinking my wine, Katharine," he urged. "But serve me some of your wine, too."

So we stood in the middle of his garden, drinking each other's wine. The wine helped us see who the other person is—and to connect with different parts of each other more deeply. After a while, David returned us to Salem's garden.

PERFECTED SOUL

By the time we stepped back in, Don and Yahweh had packed the picnic gear. Yahweh said his goodbyes, promising to return later in the book.

"Do you mind if we take the long way back to the house?" I asked Don. "I wanted to tell you how your teaching helped me in very practical ways."

"I won't argue with that," Don grinned.

"I invited David to join us," I added.

David did walk beside us. But he spent most of the time examining the flowers Salem had displayed on either side of the path. Occasionally, he'd call Don and me over to point out one that captured his attention.

"For years, I thought that it would be impossible to clear the soul of trauma fully," I told Don as we began the stroll back. "But using your tools, my soul reached a perfected state—cleared all of her trauma. Well, for two days. But seeing it happen for even a brief period has convinced me that we will clear all of our trauma permanently."

"I believe the soul not only can but will reach a state of perfection," Don agreed.

"As soon as my soul felt as powerful and perfect as my spirit, she told me, 'This is the reason I chose to exist—to feel like this, to be able to do this.' The soul doesn't exist so she can hold our trauma for us. She exists to feel perfect, amazing, and powerful—and do the list of things she wants to do. Once my soul realized she was perfect and powerful, my spirit took my soul to different realms and announced, 'This is my soul. She now realizes that she's perfect. Listen to her!' It felt like a coming-of-age thing for my soul. She was being presented in places where my spirit was taken seriously and listened to. My spirit was saying that my soul should be given the same respect."

"I'm glad to hear that, Katharine," Don smiled. "I believe you won't be the only one who experiences a deeper interaction with perfection as a result of sitting in my words."

"I agree," I nodded. "Speaking of your words producing incredible results, as I wrote down your talks in this book, something amazing happened."

"What?" Don smiled.

NEW GATE

"A gate opened in the heavens," I explained energetically. "Impressive angels stood at the gate, sounding loud trumpets as the golden, pearly gates opened. They said they had been waiting since the Beginning to open that gate for humanity. And it's now open as a result of your talks. Guess what gate it was?"

"What?"

"It's linked to the Way of Life you're speaking about tomorrow. But it's also about perfection, so I wanted to tell you now. It's a gate inside us that's also in the heavenly realms. A gate that will take us into Life and Immortality. I heard it called the Gate of Incorruptibility."

"Wow," Don whistled. "Tell me more."

"Well, tomorrow, you'll speak about the incorruptible seed we hold inside us," I explained. "You'll quote 1 Peter 1:23: 'Being born again, not of corruptible seed, but of incorruptible, by the word of God, which liveth and abideth for ever' (KJV). As I typed up your words and engaged with them, I realized that Yahweh must have breathed that seed into us in the Beginning. Yahweh's nature is incorruptible. That means it can't be corrupted. Nothing can corrupt it. He breathed that nature into *us*. So, nothing can corrupt *us*. The estate of corruption people find themselves in isn't a result of something they did. It's not the result of a thought or imagination or desire. None of that stuff can corrupt us. Nothing can corrupt us. That's what 'incorruptible' means. Our nature can't be corrupted. Can Yahweh be corrupted? Neither can we."

"So, how did we end up in an estate of corruption?" Don asked.

"The Gate of Incorruptibility would say that you're not corrupted," I replied, smiling. "It's that simple. You're like Yahweh. He can't be corrupted. Neither can the seed he put inside you."

"So, how did we end up in an estate of corruption?" Don asked again.

"You're only in an estate of corruption as long as you agree with that estate," I answered. "If you agree you're incorruptible, you leave the estate of corruption. What if we didn't inherit corruption as our nature, but we inherited a belief system—like a government structure—over our lives that tells us we're corrupted? But what if our divine nature itself was never corrupted? If you remove corruption as the belief system over your life, then you leave the estate of corruption. You enter life. I know it burns down religious doctrine. Religion tells us something is deeply wrong with us. Then it tries to fix it." I laughed. "I saw a vision of burning the buildings of religion when that gate opened. Like how Martin Luther's few suggestions nailed to a church door started a revolution, the Gate of Incorruptibility does the same thing."

"You're saying we were never messed up?"

"Don't ask *me* that question. Ask the seed inside you. Ask the incorruptible nature of God that lives inside you. Or, ask the gate. I'm sure it will speak for itself," I answered. "The truth about who we are will be fully discovered one day. We just need to know where to ask the right questions."

"That's great news, Katharine," Don mused. "I think we should open as many gates to Life as possible."

"Absolutely. Especially the ones that start revolutions," I laughed, thinking of Martin Luther and the few little points he wanted to make.

By then, we had arrived back at the house. After thanking David, Don and I parted ways to prepare for the evening's festivities.

Chapter 17

I chose a floor-length blue evening gown overlaid in sequins for the formal dinner that night. After putting the necklace on and removing it, half a dozen times, I settled on wearing my new pearl necklace. I even found the courage to slip on the earrings. Sliding into heels, I hurried downstairs. I didn't want to be the last person at the table two nights in a row.

Scurrying down the hallway, I passed scores of people. Many were guests in Salem's home like I was. But many more were coming for the events—the parties and the lectures—and returning to their own houses at night. One of the beings I passed was Righteousness. I hadn't seen him since our time on the patio the day before. He was still wearing a tux.

"Good to see you again, Righteousness," I smiled.

"Katharine, just the person I was looking for. Do you have a moment now for me to show you my message for the book?" he asked.

"Sure," I agreed, ditching my plan not to be last to dinner.

I followed him down the hallway to a door on the right. Unlocking it, he beckoned for me to enter. The room was filled with cardboard banker boxes. Some stacks reach almost to the ceiling.

"This is my room here," Righteousness announced. "I brought important documents explaining righteousness in the new era. I'm giving them to you. Read them and incorporate them in your writing."

"Wow, thanks," I whistled. "This is a lot." Instinctively, I walked to the window to take in the view. "Care to boil it down to a sentence or two?"

"Not really. I think you'll know what to do with it," he answered.

"I've been thinking about righteousness recently," I confessed. "I believe we need to align with you differently to enter this new era. I have thoughts in my head, but they get stuck there. I haven't been able to teach it."

"Maybe these documents will help," Righteousness suggested.

"Yes, thanks," I nodded. "Most of the teaching I've heard about righteousness comes from a child's perspective on what being righteous means. We need to shift to an adult mindset about righteousness to enter the new era fully.

"Jesus understood that. He approached the law like he was its source. It was there to serve him, not the other way around," I continued. "Jesus even said, 'The Sabbath was made for man, not man for the Sabbath.' The Sabbath was one of the Ten Commandments. There's a lot more there. I'd love to unpack it. We'll be able to do so much more when we understand you from an adult perspective."

When I assured Righteousness that my staff would transport these boxes to my house, he locked the door behind us. I knew that meant not everyone was ready to read his documents. There certainly were a lot of things brewing in Salem's house that hadn't been released yet.

DINNER

After saying goodbye, I hurried to dinner. Descending the curved grand staircase to the ground level, I was overcome by the majesty of the King of Salem's house.

A live band was playing in the entryway at the bottom of the stairs. Their music filled the atmosphere with an elegant, festive mood. Flowers filled urns and draped across doorways in every room. The air itself was shimmering with something like gold-infused light. Wealth and grandeur were embodied almost physically in the atmosphere. When a true king hosts a celebration, he shows no limits.

Winding through the elegant rooms, I found my place at the dinner table. Don was already seated. When he spotted my necklace and earrings, he grinned. Then, he raised one arm, revealing the pearl cufflinks. We had the same thought.

Dinner passed uneventfully. Sitting next to me this evening was Lydia from the Bible. Partway through the meal, she slipped me a note for someone on earth. "You can put the message in the book if you wish," she told me.

I opened the note to read: Keep going, and you'll get what you want.

"That's encouraging," I remarked, smiling.

"It's a great reminder for anyone who longs for a reality greater than anything that's ever been experienced before," Lydia replied.

"Sometimes, I wish it was smooth sailing straight into our dreams," I sighed.

"But then you'd stay at such a low level of dreaming," she explained. "Every dream worthy of who you are requires you to stretch to reach it. If you settled for something less, you'd be back to yearning for more soon. The fact that you don't possess all that you seek right now proves that you're stretching yourself until your reality matches your full, divine identity. You're right on track."

I examined Lydia more closely. She was a great queen now. On her fingers were more rings than I had ever seen on anyone in heaven. Her green and gold dress was as regal and costly as Salem's wardrobe. Clearly, her words carried great authority.

"Thank you," I told her, squeezing her hand in appreciation.

TIME TO DANCE

After dinner, I migrated to one of the lounges. The King of Righteousness and the King of Peace stood before an oversized stone fireplace, a fire crackling behind them. A group of ten or fifteen people sat on the plush furniture nearby, listening intently to the stories the kings shared. I joined them.

I was enthralled with the kings, the guests, and the worthiness of everything surrounding me. For example, everyone at the event had an abundance of knowledge. A five-minute conversation with anyone around me would be worth more than reading every book written on earth on whatever subject we discussed. Everyone was also fabulously wealthy. They were immensely powerful. They were perfectly humble. I felt like I was at a luxury resort for the rich, wise, and flawless. I wanted to soak in every minute with these people in this place.

Fifteen minutes after I entered the lounge with the kings, Don tapped me on the shoulder. "I've been asked to summon you," he grinned. "Someone in the ballroom is insisting on dancing with you."

"Sure," I laughed.

On the inside, the ballroom looked even more striking than the peek we had gotten from the hallway the night before. The band had moved from the entryway to the ballroom. Their music was still so perfectly in pitch that listening to it made me high.

"Who's insisting on a dance?" I asked Don after we positioned ourselves next to the refreshment table.

"He is," Don nodded at the figure approaching us enthusiastically.

"Time!" I called. "I didn't know you danced."

"There are many things I can do that you haven't yet learned about, my lady," Time replied, winking and bowing simultaneously. "Would you care to unfurl the repertoire of my abilities you haven't explored?"

"If you're asking me to dance, the answer is yes," I replied, glancing at Don and smiling.

Once on the dance floor, I sized up my partner more closely. Time was dressed entirely in off-white. His jacket was embroidered with shining white thread, revealing an elaborate pattern that glistened when it caught the light. His shoulders were broader than I recalled. Two of me could have fit in between them. Most importantly, he was a fantastic dancer.

He had a sense of rhythm and, of course, timing. He knew when to twirl me, when to dip me, and when to glide me graciously across the floor in step to the music. He also knew how to carry on a conversation while doing all that.

"What about me scares you?" Time asked.

"Nothing," I replied.

"Then open yourself up more to me," he urged. "I want a relationship with your generation, unlike the relationship past generations have had. I wasn't created to supervise children. I long for adult interaction."

"You wanted to dance, not talk," I mused. "Dancing in spiritual encounters can be a powerful experience. I teach people that if they have difficulty connecting with Yahweh, Yeshua, or Holy Spirit, they should try dancing with them. Dancing involves 'physical' touch. It involves eye contact. And it involves motion. All those things help to align us with the other person. I've never tried dancing with you, Time, but it should work the same way. Dancing forces us to align because we have to move together. Anything in me that's out of sync with who you are has to flow in harmony with you when you're gliding me across a dance floor.

"The 'physical' touch helps me connect more deeply, too. For example, if I can only see and hear Yahweh in an encounter, but I can't understand what he's thinking ten layers down, sometimes I wait to interact until I can find that deeper connection. A trick I learned that opens the deep flow is to touch his form. I'd put a hand on his face, chest, or arm. Dancing forces our hands to touch, which can spark that deeper alignment.

"Finally, dancing requires looking the other person in the eye. That's the other trick I learned that would help me connect to Yahweh beyond what I could see and hear in a vision. Dancing does all three things at once. It forces you to move together as your hands touch, and you look each other in the eye. I bet people could flow with you much more deeply by dancing with you," I added quickly. "Is that why you asked me to dance?"

"I asked you to dance for many reasons, Katharine," Time smiled, "including that I'd like to connect with other people by dancing with them. What we're doing is an example that can open that for them. But I also wanted to tell you: Open your heart to me—your heart, Katharine, not your mind. Don't try to understand me intellectually. Connect with me. I'll flow to you all the understanding you need. But I want to move it through channels you and I hand-carve."

As if to prove my point about the power of dancing in the spiritual realms, everything froze when we looked each other in the eye. It was like time stood still so the being Time could show me who he is. Time spoke to me for a million years—all in two seconds. He took me everywhere that exists, all at once. He filled my heart with laughter. Every burden lifted. There was enough time to take care of everything. Time would never run out for me. It would be my friend, my ally, my closest partner. So there was no need to worry. Didn't so much of my worry stem from believing time was limited?

"I open my heart to you," I whispered. "I want our connection to be what you want it to be, too."

As soon as I spoke those words, our dance was over. The music stopped. Like a gentleman, Time bowed.

MORE THAN TIME

Walking off the dance floor, I was still in a daze. Oblivious to my surroundings, I almost bumped into Don.

"Whoa, Katharine," he exclaimed, nearly spilling his drink. "Did you have a good time dancing? Or rather, did you have a good dance with Time?"

"Both," I laughed. "You're taking drinking seriously tonight. Double fisted."

"I grabbed a drink for myself and a friend," Don explained.

"Who's your friend?" I asked.

"Come with me and find out," Don answered.

Drinks in both hands, he forged a path through the crowd to the balcony. Outside, it was serene and uncrowded. He led us to the stone balcony overlooking the gardens and the woods beyond. Above us, a million stars twinkled. Leaning against the stone railing, a beautiful figure in a long dress was enjoying the view. When she heard us approach, she turned around.

"Wisdom!" I exclaimed as I gave her a half hug.

She kissed my cheek in greeting as she accepted the drink from Don.

"This is your friend?" I asked Don.

"She wanted to see you, Katharine," Don winked. "I promised I'd snatch you away from Time as soon as possible and lure you to the balcony so you two could chat in a quieter setting."

"Are you enjoying your time here, Katharine?" Wisdom asked.

"It's been very enlightening," I answered.

"I want you to go on more adventures with the kinds of people here," she told me.

"You belong here, Katharine," Don agreed. "You should stay. Work with us."

"Stay at Salem's place?" I laughed.

"You know what we mean. You belong in the realms like this—with the kinds of people you're meeting here, working on the projects we're doing."

"It is magical," I smiled.

I leaned against the balcony, breathing in the pure night air. Standing between Don and Wisdom on a perfect night in a perfect place, their words made sense. Maybe I should give up everything else I was doing and immerse myself in their work. I inhaled deeply, relaxing into that thought. Then, something overpowering nearly smacked me senseless.

"Oh, wow! That's—wow!" I exclaimed, trying not to swear.

"What's wrong, Katharine?" Don asked, concerned.

"I think I was standing a millimeter too close to you when I took that last deep breath. I inhaled part of who you are, and it was—" I paused to describe it. "You are overwhelmingly powerful. I thought Time's ability to navigate the heavenly realms was amazing. But you're so much more powerful than he is. There's no comparison."

Don chuckled. "Time was created to serve us. It shouldn't surprise you that a son of God is greater than Time."

"I know. I shouldn't be surprised by now," I replied.

"I understand what Katharine means," Wisdom chimed in. "When someone on earth unlocks their divine nature, they become exponentially more incredible and powerful than most people think a human on earth can be."

"Exactly," I agreed, grinning at Wisdom. "You know all about unlocking people's divine nature and how explosively powerful they can become."

"I enjoy working with people to bring them to maturity," Wisdom smiled. "Tell the people reading this book I'm more powerful and wonderful than most people realize."

PEARLS

"Those are beautiful pearls, Katharine," Wisdom changed the subject, running her fingers gently down my necklace. "May I ask where you got them?"

"We think they're connected to an artifact we uncovered in Salem's attic last night—a book tied to creation," I answered. "Don's wearing pearl cufflinks that accompany the book, too."

"We suspect the pearls contain the frequencies and secrets of the book," Don added.

"Have your pearls done anything?" Wisdom asked.

"See for yourself," Don replied, pulling back his jacket to reveal his cufflinks.

"They're talking!" I exclaimed. "They're chatting a mile a minute."

After listening for a few seconds, Wisdom declared, "They're reciting a numerical sequence."

"I know. They haven't stopped buzzing since I put them on," Don remarked.

"Are my pearls saying anything you can hear?" I asked Wisdom.

She leaned closer for several seconds, then shook her head. "But they're glowing, Katharine."

"She's right. I didn't notice it inside. But in the darkness here, it's quite obvious," Don confirmed.

Now I noticed it, too. The necklace was softly luminescent. So were the earrings, they assured me.

"I wonder what all that means," I looked at Wisdom quizzically.

She leaned over and whispered something in my ear that made me laugh.

Don just shrugged. "If she told us, Katharine, Moshe would probably explode. He wants to be the one to explain everything related to that book to us."

I shot him a look, mystified. "That's exactly what Wisdom just whispered to me."

"You two have much more to dig into on this adventure," Wisdom told us. "The pearls are just one of the treasures you'll take away from your time here. I'll never be truly apart from you. But I do have to go now."

After bidding us goodbye, Wisdom wandered off into the crowd.

MORE MYSTERIES

"Do you know what the best part about all this is?" Don asked when Wisdom disappeared.

"The food?"

"My favorite part is unveiling the mysteries," he answered.

"You want to explore the mysteries hidden in this house again," I smiled. "I can read your thoughts. You want to use the second key you gave me."

Looking at him, I could see how events could play out. We sneak to the third floor. We use the key to enter a guarded room at the end of the long hallway. It's filled with scrolls. Don pulls an oversized scroll from an urn and spreads it on the floor. It's a living map showing exactly where in all the realms you need to go to fulfill the most important thing you could be doing right now. Don and I take turns looking at the map individually. Then we look together for the work we're doing jointly.

"That would be amazingly enlightening," I nodded. "And fun. Do you think we have time to do that and still meet at the lake?"

"Probably not," he shrugged. "But did you see where you need to go on the map?"

"Yep," I smiled. "And I saw it for our work together, too. Want to know where it was?"

"Surprise me."

"Your favorite part really is the mystery," I laughed.

"Speaking of the lake, why don't you change into something more comfortable and meet me there in half an hour," Don suggested.

Chapter 18

I followed the path to the lake as Don directed. Up close, it was even more stunning. I watched as huge fish jumped from the water in search of food. Or perhaps they were greeting me.

"There you are," a voice startled me from behind. "You found it."

A figure emerged from the trees lining the bank into the moonlight.

"Yeshua!" I exclaimed. It felt so good to see him that before I realized what I was doing, I had run over to him and hugged him tightly. "I wondered why you hadn't appeared in this book. All the speakers are quoting your words. I kept waiting for you to step in."

"And here I am," he smiled.

My face was still nuzzled against his white, floor-length robe. It felt softer than I expected. As I inhaled deeply, a pleasant fragrance filled my senses. "I can smell your cologne," I told him.

As I was still acclimating to Jesus' presence, another figure stepped out of the shadows. Taking the form of a tall, attractive man, Holy Spirit stared at me. Without thinking, I let go of Jesus and took a step backward—my eyes glued to Holy Spirit the entire time. A thousand emotions flooded my mind at once. It felt overwhelmingly wonderful to see him—like a reunion with a dearest friend or relative or lover. Yet, anger, regret, and heartache surfaced, too. Unbidden, tears streamed down my cheeks. Tears formed in the edges of his eyes, too.

I didn't know if I wanted to run as fast as I could into his embrace— or refuse to embrace him at all. The first feeling won. Rushing into his arms, I sobbed until my tears ran out. "I'm so sorry," I kept telling him. "I'm so sorry. I wonder now if I should have gone."

Two or three years earlier, Holy Spirit had asked if I'd run off with him. I wasn't sure what he meant by it or if he was serious. But my answer had been that there were things on earth I still wanted to do, things that felt important. Things I wasn't sure someone else could do—not for a few generations. I wanted to do them. So I told him no. Now that I had seen how things had played out the last few years, part of me wondered if I should have said yes.

As we embraced, he was reaching inside me, asking me the same question again. Despite my sobs, despite the pull I felt towards him and the things I had endured and had left to endure, my heart gave him the same answer. There were still things on earth I wanted to do, things that felt important. I wanted to do them.

"Then go do what you came to do," he whispered. "I release you."

"You release me from what?" I asked.

"From your fears and inhibitions. You worry that you messed up the precious thing we had together by deciding to work with the people here. But you didn't. You couldn't mess up your destiny if you tried. You have many journeys ahead of you. Live them."

I stepped away from both Holy Spirit and Yeshua to collect myself. Trying to pull myself into work mode, I told them, "I was supposed to meet Don here. He had something important to tell me for the book."

"He's coming," Yeshua answered. "He asked us to meet you here first. He suggested that we do something fun with you."

"I believe his exact words were, 'Show her that building the new heaven and new earth isn't all meetings and lectures. It should be the best time of your life,'" Holy Spirit added.

"Have you ever skated on water, Katharine?" Yeshua asked, a gleam in his eye.

"Many times. I played ice hockey in high school," I grinned.

"Have you ever skated on non-frozen water?" he laughed.

"Never."

"Then you're in for a thrill. Take off your shoes. It's more fun if you feel the water on your feet," he directed.

When our shoes rested on the shoreline, he extended his hand to me and led us onto the water.

SKATING WITH THE STARS

The night sky above the lake was pitch black. In it, thousands of stars twinkled. The serene lake was a perfect reflection of them. So it felt like we were walking on water. But it looked like we were walking in the stars.

When we reached the center of the lake, we took a moment to breathe in the cosmos. It felt like we were fully surrounded by the majesty of heaven while touching the mysteries of the water's depths. That moment alone would have been enough.

Signaling me with a nod, Yeshua began gliding us across the water's surface. The stars themselves seemed to take notice of our movements. As we floated past their reflections on the water, it looked like they were bowing in reverence to us. Deep inside, I could feel their hum, acknowledging who we were. They were welcoming us into their domain as an honored king and queen. As we covered more and more of the lake's surface, greater portions of the heavens above opened to us—extending their homage.

With every glide across the water, I realized later, Yeshua was opening new realms to me. What looked like stars bowing down to us was Yeshua extending my authority in high places as he sailed us into heavenly domains.

It wasn't just the heavens above who noticed us. Salem's realm attended us, too. As we skimmed across the lake, hundreds of fireflies took flight. Swarming around us, they formed patterns in response to our movements. As we zig-zagged across the lake, our firefly escort kept pace. Watching their tiny lights flicker in response to us swelled my heart with joy. With lights above our heads, lights below our feet, and lights circling us, I felt like we were gliding through the wonder of endless lights.

After a long while, we stood quietly in the middle of the lake again. It felt like multiple realms were watching, bowing in reverence to the king and queen before them.

SOAKED

"That was amazing," I announced, breathless. Staring into the night sky, I sighed. "I could stay in this spot for a long time. Do you camp on water with people, too?"

Yeshua laughed. "Do you think there's something I couldn't do?"

"Yes," I replied. "I don't think you could be dull."

"Fair enough," he laughed.

Just then, Don skated up. He nodded to Yeshua. Then he asked, "How was your little glide across the lake?"

"Magical," I grinned.

When I saw that Don could skate on the water without holding Yeshua's hand, I asked, "Will I fall in the water if I let go of your hand? I'd like to skate around by myself, too."

"There's a way to find out," Yeshua suggested, smiling mischievously.

I positioned myself between Yeshua and Don. That way, in case I sank, I had double the chance of being rescued quickly. Then I let go. They let me sink as far as my waist before rescuing me. Letting me half drown was bad enough, as far as I was concerned. But then Yeshua gave me a two-minute lesson, and I got the hang of how to levitate on water. That only made me more furious.

"You could have given me that lesson before suggesting that I let go of you to find out if I'd sink or float," I announced, miffed. "And both of you could have rescued me before I was half soaked."

The men just looked at each other, grinning.

"You are both about to be drenched from head to toe," I swore, wobbling a bit but managing to skate close enough to kick water up as far as their knees when I skidded to a stop.

"I'm afraid you're going to be the one completely soaked," Yeshua laughed. "My mission tonight was to have fun with you. What could be more fun than this?"

And that started the water battle on the lake. We skated. We skidded. We slide-tackled each other. We were able to knock each other to the water's surface but not below. Even with the ability to not sink underwater, we all ended up drenched.

We skated as fast as we could, scooping a hand through the water to spray another person as we passed them. We skidded at someone's feet, smacking them onto the water's surface. We didn't stop when our opponents were completely soaked. We kept drenching each other until we laughed so hard we could barely keep our balance skating.

SUNRISE

Soaked and laughing, we were racing around in the middle of the lake when we first noticed it. Ever since my dance with Time, I had lost track of time. I wasn't sure when I had arrived at the lake. I wasn't sure how long Yeshua and I spent gliding across its surface. I wasn't sure how long we had been drenching each other afterward. But one thing was certain. The sun was peeking over the horizon.

As the early rays skimmed across the lake and hit us, Don announced, "A new day is dawning for humanity. We get to be part of it."

Instinctively, we turned to face the dawn. Watching the sunrise anywhere is stunning. Watching the sunrise as you hover millimeters above the water on a mystical lake is a thousand times more breathtaking. But watching this sunrise on this lake—in the King of Salem's world—

held special significance. Salem had tuned everything about his realm to helping humanity build the new heaven and new earth. His sun rising over his lake carried the frequency of hope and life and abundance and change.

When the sunrise began, Yeshua was standing between Don and me. As the sun's rays hit me, I looked over to Yeshua. But he had disappeared. Only Don's figure remained on the lake with me. But I felt another divine spirit's presence behind us. Without turning around, I knew it was Holy Spirit. Silently and majestically, he extended his essence to hover over us.

As the sun hit my being, with Holy Spirit's essence like a canopy above me, I came alive. Soon, I flowed in heavenly sync with everything around me—from the light to the water to the divine essence near me. Every molecule in my being surged with delight and hope. I wanted that feeling to go on forever. I wanted to build the new heaven and new earth in that feeling and through that feeling. I realized it couldn't be built any other way.

"Forming the new heaven and new earth isn't about following a blueprint," I whispered to Don as a profound realization hit me. "It's about what's happening inside us now, isn't it? We get transformed from the inside out. We feel abundant life and joy and love and provision inside us first. We flow in our divine nature—through the divine nature of the Trinity. Then, we build in that frequency. If we try to build from any other foundation, it will crumble. What's circulating between us and Holy Spirit and creation right now—that joy, delight, hope, peace, love—that's the most important thing. Everything else is built from that. I knew that in my head. But feeling it here is taking that truth deeper."

"Good," Don nodded. "That's what I wanted to show you at the lake."

Day 3

Chapter 19

I missed breakfast again. When the Spirit of God flows through you in a way that makes you feel like *this* is the meaning of life, it's hard to want to do something as mundane as eat breakfast. I even missed the breakfast spread for late risers. But I was so high I didn't care. I wasn't hungry.

My schedule for the day was all meetings. One-on-one meetings, mostly. I was surprised to see another session of the Distribution Committee on my schedule. When I ran into Don in the hall, he told me he had more of the same, too. Meetings and lectures. I told him I planned to attend his second talk. But I had a full schedule before then.

"By the way, I think I figured out why we've had days *and* nights full of unpacking mysteries," I told Don before we parted ways for the day's adventures.

"Really? Why?" he grinned like he already knew.

"I've heard Ian say that daytime is for the revelation of mysteries. We can think about and understand mysteries with all our cognitive senses then," I explained. "He says nighttime is for entering the mysteries of Yahweh. The purpose of night isn't to sleep. It's to explore the kinds of mysteries of Yahweh that can't be explored during daylight hours when our bodies and minds are in a different state. At Salem's house, that's what we've been doing, Don. We haven't been sleeping at night. Well, maybe I dozed in the attic. But otherwise, we've been entering into Yahweh's mysteries at night. It wasn't a coincidence Moshe took us to the attic at night to encounter Yahweh's voice at creation. It wasn't a coincidence that Yeshua led me over the depths of the waters and the stars at night—or that we watched the sunrise with Holy Spirit to grasp that profound mystery. Those were things that can only be fully discovered in the watches of the night."

"It *is* odd that we haven't slept during this visit," Don remarked.

"Not odd—symbolic. I think Salem is signaling that there are mysteries so deep here that some of them must be entered into at night," I announced. "Or maybe his place is just so full of mysteries that we could explore it 24 hours a day and not come to the end of it."

"I think you're right, Katharine. If we keep our exploration of heaven's mysteries to daylight hours only, we will miss a lot."

"On earth, many of my encounters are during the day. But often, my deepest revelations are at night. I rarely sleep the entire night. I'm in encounters just about every night. Same with you."

"The night watches are important," Don nodded.

"Now that we've figured that out, I need to hurry toward unpacking my daytime mysteries," I laughed. "I do have a full schedule before your talk."

"So do I," Don sighed. "But aren't full schedules the best?"

"Around here they are," I winked. "You never know what's in store."

ENOCH

People like Enoch were taking one-on-one sessions in their guest quarters at Salem's house. When I entered, he was pouring us drinks. I could tell he was enjoying a day filled with private, meaningful chats. He was dressed in formal clothes—in the same style the kings and Melchizedek wore. It was perhaps the most distinguished-looking I had ever seen him.

"What message did you have for the book?" I asked.

"All in good time," he answered. "Let's catch up first."

After asking about some things I was working on privately, he announced, "You're like me, Katharine. If you apply yourself to these things you're looking into, you can impact humanity in monumental ways."

"Is that what you did—impact humanity monumentally? I thought you left us to follow your own pursuits," I replied politely.

"My defiance of death has inspired many to pursue immortality—yourself included," he answered. "But you're right. My biggest contribution to humanity is opening now. I'll be a much greater figure a hundred years from now than I am presently. My influence will continue to grow. The same can be true of you and anyone like you."

"Is that your message for this book?" I asked.

"No, those are my words to you personally, words that apply to anyone who believes them," he answered. "For the book, I want to tell people to keep going. The end is within reach. Don't stop pursuing the things of this new era just because they seem unbelievable or unattainable. Believe it or not, there will come a day when it will seem more reasonable to believe in immortality than to dismiss it. There will be a day when children will have to be taught what death was. It will be a lesson in school—like learning about polio or another illness that's been eradicated. Teachers will explain what funerals were and why inheritance laws were written assuming elders would die. The whole system will seem silly and foreign to your children."

"Like the laws of colonial America, forbidding people from taking their lions into town unless they were leashed?" I grinned. "Children will laugh at our current legal system, wondering what in the world society must have looked like to have laws like that?"

"Legal codes will be rewritten assuming life, not death," Enoch continued. "At first, the law will change to acknowledge that not everyone will die. There will be two ways of providing for descendants—transfers triggered when the elder dies and transfers triggered by qualifying events in the children's lives. That way, you'll be able to leave money to your children at milestones in their lives without your death triggering the money transfer."

"Makes sense," I nodded.

"You understand that part because you were a lawyer. But you won't be involved in rewriting the laws. Others will do that part," Enoch continued. "There's much that will change. Write that down. Think about how much of society now is centered around death, disease, poverty, hurt, and pain. As those things are lifted from humanity, every single thing about life and society will be restructured.

"My main point now is to raise people's hopes and expectations," Enoch summarized, "I want as many people as possible to see, understand, and work for the monumental changes that are coming."

METATRON

I closed Enoch's door behind me and hurried downstairs. A one-on-one meeting with the angel Metatron was next on my schedule. In a spare study, he had set up a makeshift office to meet with people. When I entered the room, he was pacing, his gorgeous purple and gold robe flowing gracefully behind him.

"Thanks for taking the time to interview me," he began. "People have misunderstood me. They've judged me. You found that to be the case, didn't you, when you researched me?"

A few weeks before this interview, Metatron asked me to research something about him. In my hunt, I discovered numerous websites denouncing him as demonic. About the same time, a friend told me of an insightful Christian teacher who had recently issued a similar warning.

"I've never encountered anything off about Metatron," I assured my friend. "But I wouldn't be surprised if there are counterfeit 'Metatrons.' Other spirits may use his name to convince people to partner with them.

That would make sense to me that some clever spirits would do that."

Now, I was standing next to the genuine Metatron in the King of Salem's house. How can you tell the fake from the genuine? Time always tells—not the being Time—but the true nature of any spirit over time becomes apparent. Is it leading you into life? Into holiness? Into freedom and all the other virtues that stem from our divine nature? Or is it fostering fear, condemnation, shame, and the other things that corruption produces?

Personally, I had no reservations about interacting with Metatron.

"I'm glad to hear that, Katharine," he smiled, reading my thoughts. "What did your research find about me?"

"Some people believe you're the angel in Exodus 23:20–21—the one Yahweh sent to guide Israel through the desert, the one who taught Moshe the ways of Yahweh, the one who Yahweh said his name is in. From what I've seen of you, that makes sense," I answered.

"Good," Metatron chuckled gently. "I've kept myself hidden over the epochs, but not anymore. I'll move to the forefront more now. Tell people why."

"I suspect the reason is that you have an important role in building the new heaven and new earth," I replied. "Some people believe you assisted Yahweh at creation, witnessing the original thoughts and designs from which everything was formed. You've guarded countless mysteries about creation and life over the eons. It would make sense that you'd have a major role in the new heaven and earth."

Metatron smiled. "I want to work with people. But I don't work with anybody and everybody—not closely. Yes, people call on my energy or what I've released to creation. They can do that and see results. But that's not the same as working with me. I've come to this conference to recruit people to work with me. Do you understand?"

"I think so. You want a partnership with people."

"I've been waiting for humanity to mature enough to work with me face to face and not in riddles," Metatron answered.

It reminded me of how Yahweh said he revealed himself to prophets in dreams and visions. But not with Moshe. "With him I speak face to face, clearly and not in riddles; he sees the form of the LORD" (Num. 12:8 NIV). Did Metatron speak with Moshe face to face and not in riddles? Did Moshe see Metatron—and in doing so, see the form of Yahweh—a reflection or encasing of his nature?

CLOSER LOOK

"Put your hand on my heart, Katharine. I want to show you some things about me," Metatron directed.

When my fingers glazed his outer robe, I realized it was thicker than it appeared from a distance. "You're truly majestic," I whispered in awe.

"Thank you," he smiled involuntarily.

He opened himself to me for several minutes, showing me different aspects of who he is and what he knows.

"Wow!" I exclaimed, stepping back and looking at him in wonder. "You have more of Yahweh's nature on you than any angel I've met! No wonder Yahweh said his name was in you (Ex. 23:21). No wonder you're identified as the angel of his Presence (Ex. 33:14). Rabbinic tradition says you're the only angel allowed to sit down in Yahweh's presence in heaven. I didn't believe those reports until I breathed you in just now. You're more than those sources claimed you to be!"

Metatron was modest. "I think people should form their own opinions of me," he replied. "Don't take anyone's word for it. Come to know me yourself."

I looked at him in wonder, eager to continue our interaction. But the interview was over. "Hurry to Don's lecture, Katharine. You and I both have things to do there," he winked.

Chapter 20

Don was scheduled for another talk before lunch. At Metatron's urging, I entered the waiting room early. I didn't want to miss a thing. Choosing a chair closer to the door, I caught every word Don spoke—uninterrupted.

"I'm going to share three important things about the Way of Life," Don began. "This isn't the way of the Tree of Life. That's a function. This is the Way of Life itself. This pathway will lead you to sovereignty."

DEATH

"My journey on this pathway began when I realized that I was literally ready to die for Christ," Don continued. "I realized that if someone had a gun to my family members and I had the option to save their lives at the cost of my own, I was ready to die. The posture of my heart into death opened up the doorway into sovereignty. Only the one who is ready to die can walk into sovereignty.

"That's not just my own experience. That's what the Bible says. Yeshua declared that 'unless a kernel of wheat falls to the ground and dies, it remains only a single seed. But if it dies, it produces many seeds. Anyone who loves their life will lose it, while anyone who hates their life in this world will keep it for eternal life' (John 12:24–25 NIV). Paul said, 'I die daily' (1 Cor. 15:31 KJV).

"If a seed dies, it brings forth much fruit," Don explained. "Yeshua entered eternal life by being willing to lay down his life in death. Paul lived in that same posture every day. We need to be positioned so we can learn, like Paul did, how to die daily so that out of that death, life can be produced. We have the incorruptible seed of life inside us. When we are willing to lay our lives down, that seed opens. It opens to bear the fruit of eternal life.

"Peter writes about the incorruptible seed inside us. He says that we are 'born again, not of corruptible seed, but of incorruptible, by the word of God, which liveth and abideth for ever' (1 Pet. 1:23 KJV). What Yahweh was entrusted with life in Origins, we possess inside us. We are the ones who are destined for that incorruptible seed of life to grow inside us until we actually look like Yahweh."

THE BEING LIFE

"Farther along my journey on the Way of Life, I met Life the being," Don continued. "The Bible says that those who find the Spirit of Wisdom, find Life (Prov. 8:35). I met Wisdom. And she introduced me to Life. Life is incredible. She expresses herself in a feminine form. She's a beautiful being that comes out of Origins.

"After sitting with her for two years, I discovered a seat within her being where she becomes a cube. And sitting within it, you come to understand life. But sitting in it also exposes another seat. It exposes the seat of corruption," Don explained. "Because you have to taste and see the real for it to expose what the counterfeit and corrupt looks like.

"When I sat with her, embracing life, I realized I was in the realm of Light. Life and Light are connected. John knew this. He wrote, 'In him was life, and that life was the light of all mankind' (John 1:1 NIV).

"We need to choose life. I can't stress enough how important it is to choose life. I have a lot of things I could share with you. I have a lot of things to speak about in the arena of finances because of some major things that have been happening. But this is what urgently needs to be said because when you walk through this stuff, you realize that we are meant to be like Yeshua. And embodying life that was the light of the world is one of the most important things Yeshua did."

BENCH OF THREE

Don paused to assess the audience. In the waiting room, some stood from their chairs and paced. I wasn't at the door peeking into the other room like Timotheus was. But I could sense the presence of huge angels. Something was opening for humanity.

"Sitting in Life, you learn what is governing you currently," Don resumed. "You see what estate we need to walk out of. It's called the estate of corruption. It can be summed up as the lust of the eyes, the lust of the flesh, and the pride of life. The Bible says, 'For all that is in the world, the lust of the flesh, and the lust of the eyes, and the pride of life, is not of the Father, but is of the world. And the world passeth away, and the lust thereof: but he that doeth the will of God abideth for ever' (1 John 2:16–17 KJV).

I saw where Don was going with this. In society, we set up a framework of laws that govern a territory. Then, we appoint judges to enforce those laws. In the biblical culture, a bench of three judges ruled in most everyday matters. Only national or regional matters had benches or courts of more than three. We do the same thing with our lives. Whether we realize it or not, we've set up rules or laws that become a framework through which everything in our lives is filtered. Then, we set up a bench of three judges to enforce those rules—to ensure we filter every experience and every understanding of ourselves through the framework.

"If corruption is the estate we're living from," Don continued, "then the bench of three over our lives can be described as the lust of the eyes, the lust of the flesh, and the pride of life. Those three things sit as judges. They make sure we filter everything through corruption. They ensure we feel things like guilt, condemnation, and unworthiness. They constantly issue rulings declaring us corrupted, disqualified, and less than Yahweh.

"The bench of three sits at the top of our scroll and its seals. Its rulings impact everything we can do with our lives and our scrolls. When the bench of corruption sits over our lives, it limits us from perfection and sovereignty.

"So we need to replace the bench of corruption. We can start by replacing it with what people have taught as 'plumblines.' Here are some of them:

- Justice, Judgment, Holiness
- The Way, The Truth, The Life
- Righteousness, Joy, and Peace
- In him I live, I move, I have my being

"Those are great things to have as a bench of three judges over our lives instead of the bench of corruption. But, ultimately, we want to replace corruption with a full expression of the divine nature:

- Omniscience, Omnipotence, Omnipresence

"Just as he is, so are we in this world," Don declared, referring to 1 John 4:17. This is what perfection looks like to the mature—fully reflecting every aspect of Yahweh's divine nature."

When Don spoke the last sentence, clapping erupted. Curious, I hurried to the door and peeked around Timotheus to see what was happening. As I suspected, it wasn't the audience clapping. It was the angels in the room. Heaven was ringing their applause. Creation really was waiting for the Sons of God to be revealed—fully revealed as reflecting Yahweh's nature in every way.

METATRON

As I returned to my seat, Timotheus whispered loudly, "The angel Metatron is walking around as Don's talking."

Three seconds later, Don announced it, too. "Metatron has been very present," Don told the audience. "He's carrying keys, dangled from his belt. He's looking to and fro for the ones to assign some of these keys."

I glanced at the chair where Metatron was sitting in the waiting room. He smiled at me, moving his robes so I could see his keys. I remembered the deafening ring they emitted when he had risen from his seat yesterday. I smiled back at him. It was still weird for me to see him here while he was also in the other room. Omnipresence takes some getting used to, I guess.

When I smiled at him, he rose from his chair and moved to one closer to me. "Do you want to know what my keys are?" he whispered loudly.

"Sure," I grinned.

Moving his outer robe, he revealed a huge set of keys—almost innumerable. "I have some keys for you, Katharine," he told me, smiling broadly. "Do you want them now?"

"Alright," I answered as I watched him remove a few keys from his belt. But he didn't hand the keys to me. Like magic, they appeared on a belt around my waist where some other keys had already rested. The keys Metatron had given me sparkled, emitting tiny particles (or perhaps beings) of light.

Leaning in, he whispered, "Light and Truth. You remember that motto. It's a Bible verse."

Yale University's motto is "Lux et Veritas"—Latin for "Light and Truth." It was taken from Psalm 43:3: "Send out your light and your truth; let them guide me. Let them lead me to your holy mountain, to the place where you live" (NLT).

"Light and Truth, Katharine," Metatron beamed. "That's a new life verse for you. You liked your old life verse, didn't you? 'Know ye not that ye are the temple of God and that the Spirit of God dwelleth in thee?' (1 Cor. 3:16 KJV). You took that verse to its fullest meaning—into union with God. Now take your new life verse. Unlock Light and Truth. Use them to guide people into every mystery until you come to the holy mountain and fully reflect all that dwells there."

Metatron's words cut deep. When I looked up the words translated "lux et veritas" in Hebrew, I realized it was "urim" and "thummim," sometimes translated as "lights" and "perfections." Those were the two stones the priest cast in the Old Testament to discern the will of Yahweh. They functioned like an oracle—revealing the thoughts, ways, and desires of God.

Did Metatron have the keys to lights? To perfections? To truths? When Moshe asked Yahweh to "show me your ways," did Yahweh send Metatron to teach him (Ex. 33:13)? Was Metatron now handing out keys that would unlock the same mysteries?

Metatron smiled. "I'm at this conference not only to hand out keys, but also to walk with the people I give them to."

"You'll tutor people?"

"I will. I will do far more than that. Tutoring is the lowest level of walking with someone. You know the higher ways," he answered. "I'm here to offer you that kind of relationship with me."

"Where you walk side by side, not just so you can be tutored, but so you come into total agreement, full attunement with the other?" I asked. "'Can two walk together unless they be agreed?' (Amos 3:3 KJV). You want to walk with people to bring us into full agreement with who you are. That means seeing, knowing, touching, and tasting every part of you. And you have a lot of knowledge. Moshe spent time with you and wrote about the Beginning from the perspective of being there himself. Did you take him to all those places? Did you show him all those things? Did he taste your essence and imbibe all those mysteries?"

Metatron laughed deeply. "I'll do more for you than I did for Moshe."

"I have no doubt you will because we will have a different relationship than you had with him," I answered confidently. "I sense you want this even more than my conscious mind does."

He turned his head away from me slightly. "You perceive correctly. I'll let you finish writing."

When Metatron rose from his chair, waves of power flowed from him in all directions. As they hit me, I had a taste of him. Mystery swirled with frequencies of tremendous volume and strength. One nanometer of his power could not just move a mountain. It could blow a mountain entirely away. And yet a tiny doorway at the center of that power— marked in darkness—beckoned me. It was an invitation to where he kept his knowledge, his power, and the chambers of his heart.

I thought I was caught up in Metatron's waves for a few seconds. But when my attention returned to the waiting room, everyone was gone. How long had I been entranced with him? I had missed people's reaction to Don's second talk.

As I stood, I noticed a piece of paper on the floor. It was a page from the book Melchizedek had been taking notes in. It must have been torn from his book. Or did he leave it for me? Salvaging it from the floor, I read Melchizedek's assessment of the talk: "Something shifted for humanity," he scribbled on his pad. "The Way of Life opened more fully." I smiled. But it was the last sentence that made my heart soar: "Soon, earth will be flooded with people of Life—with a whole generation who will never taste death."

Chapter 21

I decided to skip lunch again. This time, I strolled through the woods that bordered the house. A wide, well-maintained path meandered through the trees. Birds chirped in pleasant songs, filling my heart with joy.

Ten minutes into my stroll, I ran into Don and Yahweh. They must have been deep in conversation. Don had a serious, reverent look on his face. I couldn't see Yahweh's form, which was unusual for me. But I could feel his presence beside Don. They invited me to join them.

As Yahweh led us deeper into the woods, I whispered to Don, "I feel how much Yahweh admires you. He has a reverent respect for you. I've never perceived him feeling that way about anyone. I'm not saying you're the only one he admires like that. I'm just saying this is the first time I've witnessed him feeling that way."

"I know how he feels about me," Don nodded.

PROMISES

Yahweh led us beside a small brook and motioned for us to sit on the ground. When we were settled, he joined us. The brook gurgled in front of us, behind Yahweh's back.

"I'm sorry I frightened you the other night, Katharine," Yahweh spoke soothingly.

"The experience with you was worth the terror it caused," I assured him. "Why can't I see you now? I'm used to seeing a form for you. It's unsettling."

"I'm unlocking new ways you can understand me," Yahweh replied. "It will take some adjustment. But then you'll do fine. Open your mouth."

I looked at him quizzically for a moment, but then I complied. With a fork, he placed a generous bite into my mouth.

"What do you taste?" he asked.

"Very moist yellow cake with white icing. It's a wedding cake," I reported. "And it's delicious."

"That's the first taste of what I promise you is coming," Yahweh replied.

Trying to figure out what he meant, I said, "People often call their wedding day the best day of their lives. The wedding day of the earth is coming, isn't it? It will be the best 'day'—the best period of time—the earth has ever known."

"Very good, Katharine," Yahweh answered. "But I'm making that promise to you personally. The best 'day' of your life is coming. What you've worked and traded your entire life to possess is about to open for you."

Turning to Don, Yahweh took out a gold wedding band and slipped it on his finger. "With this ring, I thee wed," Yahweh spoke. "I will bring you into deeper union with me. I promise to show you parts of myself that I've never shown anyone before."

AS HE IS

"Those are my promises to you separately," Yahweh explained. "I want to make some promises to you together. Both of you, extend your hands towards me," Yahweh commanded.

So we reached our arms out in front of us—towards the brook. When we did, Yahweh spoke in the voice of a commanding, compassionate father, "Learn what this means: 'One can chase a thousand. And two can put ten thousand to flight' (Deut. 32:30). Together, you can open things on earth a generation sooner than it would otherwise."

After he spoke, Yahweh breathed onto our outstretched arms. His breath jolted something inside me. Then, Don's form half disappeared. I could see through his form into his spirit being.

As I was peering into Don's true identity, Yahweh whispered in my ear. "I want you to see who Don is. Then, I want you to share it with the world. He will be the first of humanity to unlock certain divine attributes fully."

At that point, Yahweh and Don sat to my left and right, facing each other. Suddenly, I became aware that the qualities inside Yahweh were beginning to be reflected in Don. He was taking on a fuller and fuller expression of who Yahweh is. Don's teaching on sovereignty unlocked for me on a deeper level. I had always thought we could partially reflect Yahweh. But, deep down, I doubted that we'd ever be able to reflect him *fully*. Now Yahweh had whispered that Don would be the first person to fully reflect certain parts of who Yahweh is. That meant other people would be the first to reflect other parts of Yahweh's nature fully. But Yahweh had no doubt that we'd completely reflect who he is one day. The Bible says that as he is, so are we in this world (1 John 4:17). The path to sovereignty is a journey to fulfill that Bible verse. We'll fully reflect him. The process I saw begin inside Don would one day reach its fullness.

QUANTUM ENTANGLEMENT

After spending a few more minutes with us, Yahweh stood to leave. But neither Don nor I felt like heading back to the conference yet. As we sat listening to the brook gurgle, I decided to probe deeper into his unmatched connection with Yahweh. He had a stronger, more vibrant relationship with him than anyone I had met.

"How did you get so close to Yahweh, Don?" I asked.

"Many things," he answered nonchalantly.

"Give me one thing you did that made a huge difference."

"Quantum entanglement," Don replied.

"I know quantum entanglement is a phenomenon that occurs in nature. Is there a way to do it in the spiritual realm, too?" I asked.

"Absolutely," Don answered. "Scientifically, quantum entanglement is defined as particles that remain intimately linked to each other even when separated by vast distances. When two particles are quantumly entangled, a change in one will affect the other—even if they are separated by billions of years of space."

"Wow," I whistled. "So it's possible to quantumly entangle with Yahweh spiritually?"

"Absolutely. The concept is in the Bible. For example, David says, 'Where can I go from your spirit? Where can I flee from your presence? If I ascend into heaven, you are there. If I make my bed in hell, you are there. If I take the wings of the morning and ascend, if I settle on the far side of the sea, even there your hand will guide me, your right hand will hold me fast' (Ps. 139:7–10 NIV).

"David was a forerunner who understood what it meant to be quantumly entangled with the God of the Universe," Don continued. "He realized that no matter where he went, he could see the face of Yahweh. They were entangled. When he saw something move in Yahweh, it also moved in him. That's what it means to be entangled."

"David wrote: 'Even there your hand shall lead me and your right hand shall hold me (Ps. 139:10). Often, when scripture says something is held, it's talking about the ability to be quantumly entangled and then to be woven together for eternity."

"I didn't realize that," I nodded, excited. "Where else in the Bible is that mentioned?"

"Solomon says about Wisdom: 'She is a tree of life for all those who hold her. Happy are those who retain her' (Prov. 3:18). Solomon was quantumly entangled with Wisdom. So she took him to where she was established and to before the Beginning when everything was made known to humanity. And he stood in the Gateway of Creation where it says, 'Let there be Light.' Through entanglement, he could be part of what Yahweh spoke as he created."

"Through entanglement, Wisdom or Yahweh can take you places spiritually?" I asked.

"Yes, and much more than that," Don explained. "Since Solomon was entangled with Wisdom, anything that moved in her also began moving in him. What's inside Wisdom? 'In her left hand is length of days. In her right hand are riches and honor' (Prov. 3:16). How did Solomon build one of the earth's wealthiest, most impressive kingdoms ever known? Did his success appear out of thin air? Or had he entangled with Wisdom, who had the treasuries of riches and honor? Every time he understood something in her, the same thing began to move in him. Because of their entanglement, it didn't matter how far they were separated—by time or space."

"Is the same true with Yahweh? When we entangle with him, then anytime we understand something about him, the same thing begins to move in us?" I wondered.

"Yes, of course."

"Then quantum entanglement is a powerful tool for spiritual growth," I concluded. "I have much less experience with quantum entanglement than you do. But I know that it creates a connection between each of your particles and each of the other's particles."

"That's right," Don nodded. "When you quantumly entangle, you walk through the fire, breaking yourself into millions of particles. So does Yahweh. Then you connect strand by strand, atom by atom, particle by particle, entangled. You flow together in that entangled state."

"It's more than a mechanical connection," I realized. "Spiritually, entanglement allows you to touch as much of the other spirit as they open to you. In theory, you could access everything about them. That's why quantumly entangling with Yahweh or Wisdom can open all their knowledge, all of their hearts, and all of their essence to you. While you're entangled, it's impossible not to be in unity with the other spirit. Every atom of yours is bound to every atom of theirs. You can align your mindsets and your heart to Yahweh's. You can take Yahweh's view of you deep into your core."

I stretched my legs out until my feet dangled over the stream bank. "Who should we quantumly entangle with?" I asked him.

"Yahweh and the whole Trinity. Wisdom," Don answered. "I see precedent for quantumly entangling with them in scripture."

After chatting a little longer, Don and I followed the trail through the woods back to the house. We both had busy agendas for the afternoon.

Chapter 22

A tour of the city of Salem was on my schedule for today. When I arrived at the gate, I was struck by the bright light emanating from the city. For a minute, it blinded me. The light itself was alive, singing at a frequency of life, joy, and power. When its rays hit my skin, love and happiness exploded inside me. Instantly, I wanted earth to shine with that kind of light.

Then I noticed the air. I inhaled wealth and prosperity with every breath, overflowing with joy and peace. A gentle breeze brushed my face. Like the air, it was alive. The breeze welcomed me to the city. It let me know the king was glad I was here. The city would embrace me. "Please come in," the breeze communicated without words. "You are welcome and honored here."

Smiling, I gazed at the gate. Several stories high, its bars were also sending out a message. They sang of how strong and worthy the city is. Mixed with their song was a personal greeting to me. I was welcome and worthy, they hummed. The light shining from the center of the city was so intense that it made the city walls and gate look bright white. But I suspected the building material was pure gold. Or perhaps the city was built from light itself.

As I peered at the gate, three beings emerged. The one in the middle was slightly ahead of the other two. When they drew near, I realized Majesty was leading the way. Glory was to his left. Worth stood on his right.

When they were a few feet from me, they stopped. Bowing on one knee, Majesty lay a box before me. It was an official gift from the city. Ceremoniously, he opened it. A large key to the city rested inside.

I thanked the delegation profusely. "But I thought the gate was open. Can't anyone come in?" I asked.

"This key both locks and unlocks," Majesty answered. "And it works inside the city walls, too. You can lock certain areas of the city to the public if you wish. Or you may unlock mysteries and hidden things in the city. You're being given limited authority over the revelation that the city contains. The king trusts you to use your authority wisely."

"Let's go in, then, and give people who can't see as well a look around," I smiled. "Let's unlock today."

"Yes, your majesty," he answered, bowing slightly.

CITY OPENING

Following my three escorts, I entered the city. The brilliant light shining from the city's center still overpowered my vision. So when I heard the noise of a band resounding, I thought at first a marching band lined the streets. But I soon realized the bricks themselves were saluting as we passed. In the brilliant light, the stones in streets and sidewalks looked pure white. But I suspected they were made of gold.

Like everything else in the city, the bricks were alive. As I stepped on them, they interfaced with my feet. Every step was an exchange between who I am and what the city is. Its blueprint was housed in every brick.

So, the further I marched into the city, the more the city became aware of me. Like a root system under a tree, the bricks I stepped on passed along my code to everything they were connected to. The city came alive to who I am, waking up and responding to me.

The city awakens to its visitors according to who the visitor is. In that sense, the city is a thoughtful, perceptive host. It won't serve chocolate cake to those who prefer vanilla. It won't open a building or share a secret if you are not interested in it or if something else would be more profitable for you to observe. Its wonders open in a way tailored to who you are.

So the city was reading the record of my life. It assessed my scrolls, my interests, and what I was ready to see and process. And it was awakening the parts of the city that were excited to interact with me. The streets burst into color, shaping themselves in a way that would best convey the information the city wanted to share with me—and you—on this visit.

ANCIENT PROPHECY

The only other heavenly city I had been in was Zion. As we passed buildings on the right and left, I thought about how similar Salem felt to Zion. Together, we followed the main street as it methodically wound up a hill towards the city center.

Shopkeepers and their customers began filing out of the buildings we passed to stare at us on our ascent. The Songs of Ascent in the Psalms came to mind. Scholars believe pilgrims sang Psalms 120–134 as they wound up Jerusalem's streets to worship in the temple. It felt like the words of those songs were resounding in the hearts of the people standing on the side of the road, watching our ascent. But they weren't singing the words to Yahweh. They looked to me and the others attending the events at the King of Salem's house to fulfill their desires.

Their hearts were positioned towards me in reverent expectation. To them, our journey to Salem's center wasn't a run-of-the-mill tour. It was a holy moment. It was the fulfillment of ancient prophecy. With the arrival of the people of "the end," we could all return to "the beginning," the prophecy had predicted.

I gleaned that information from reading the minds of the people we passed. They wondered if this march signaled the beginning of the people of "the end" pouring into their city. No one spoke. Their mouths remained shut, their faces expressionless. But their hearts burst with curiosity.

PURE IN HEART

Then, a child broke the silence. She pointed at me and exclaimed, "I see her heart, Mommy, and it's pure! You said when the pure of heart march into this city, what we do will change. Will it change now, Mommy?"

"Hush," her mother answered. "The elders will decide if her heart is pure. We won't celebrate until they announce their decision."

"But it is pure!" the child insisted loudly. "You taught me how to judge, and I can see."

"We can all see, child," the mother replied. "But we must wait for the elders. That is how the law is written."

Continuing to read their collective thoughts, I understood a basic outline of the city's history—and ultimate purpose. Salem had been founded long before records were kept marking the passage of time. The king had formed it for his own ancient purposes. But the city shone so brightly that it had been elevated to an even higher purpose. The people in the city would preserve its wealth and majesty. They were tasked with keeping its light shining, its streets spotless, and its glory unparalleled. Then, when the time was right, the city would step into its higher purpose. The job of the people in the city would shift from preserving the city's splendor to exporting the blueprints of how its wealth, glory, and majesty were generated. Some of the city's inhabitants would move outside the city walls to help other places in creation implement what Salem had crafted.

How would the inhabitants know when this shift would happen? The sign would be the arrival of a certain kind of person into the city. The people were described as the "pure in heart." They were also called the "people of the end." Most interpreted these prophecies to mean that people who were pure in heart would arrive at the end of a particular epoch. They had overcome the corruption that encased creation. They would restore creation to its former glory, which Salem had preserved.

Did that child believe I was one of the people in the city's prophecies? Was I?

KING OF SALEM

My escorts led me to the palace. It lay at the top of a hill. The bright light that nearly blinded me seemed to be coming from behind the palace. As we drew nearer, I realized the light shone from the King of Salem's heart. The city projected outward what he held in his deepest places. The palace was a "physical" representation of his heart. By walking in it, you could touch aspects of his worth and character—the qualities he built the city from.

Guards moved aside when Majesty approached the palace gates. As we passed, they saluted.

"The king wants to see you," Majesty announced, "in his private chambers."

My escorts directed me to the king's door and left. Alone with the king, I thought he looked even more regal in his city than in his house. The light was so bright that it prevented me from seeing much of our surroundings.

"What do you think of my city, Katharine?" the king asked. I think he was pouring drinks. But it was hard to tell with the brilliant light.

"From what I've seen, it's delightful," I replied. "Should I turn the light down so I can see better? Or would that reduce the amount of illumination shining into our interactions?"

"Keep the lights on, I say," Salem replied. "Here's a drink for you. Let me describe things verbally if you can't see them."

"Sure," I nodded.

"You walked into the city past the Stones of Understanding. They read what's inside whoever enters the gates. Then, they proclaim it out loud. That way, everyone in the city knows what kind of person has arrived and can act accordingly. When people heard your worth announced, they left their shops to watch you.

"To your eyes, the buildings along the main street would appear colorful. They're mostly three-story-tall townhouses. Public buildings like a library and town hall are also on that street. If you follow Main Street to the end, it takes you near the palace. Did you like your escort? I sent them myself," the king finished with a smile.

"It was all delightful," I replied. As I listened to his description, I could see more of the city in my mind. It was like someone had stopped shining a flashlight in my eyes. I could also feel the city's corporate response to me. Delighted I was there, its essence touched mine with warmth, excitement, and anticipation.

"There'll be a formal dinner in the city tonight," Salem continued. "Everyone at the conference will come here. I want to display the glory of my city to them in an official, public way."

"Will dinner include me being publicly examined by the elders for the purity of my heart?" I asked.

Salem laughed. "Hardly. What did you think of that old prophecy? Clever way to prepare people for what's coming, don't you think?"

"What does the prophecy mean?" I asked.

"Oh, it's up for interpretation," Salem answered mysteriously. "Do you think you've overcome the corruption in creation?"

"Yes and no," I replied. "I am pure in heart. But not all of me believes that."

Salem laughed heartily. "You're what we're looking for, Katharine—nothing more and nothing less. If you were more aware of your purity, you'd be sitting next to Yahweh doing what the sovereigns do. If you had less awareness of yourself, you'd be stuck in your lower states, spinning your wheels. You're ready to work with me." He stepped closer and spoke compellingly, "You're going to have the best time of your life working with me."

"Really?" I smiled. "What makes you so sure?"

"A year from now you won't ask me questions like that."

Something about how he spoke made me excited about what lay ahead.

"Put this in your book," Salem continued. "I intend to have a close relationship with a lot of people. With some people, I will be very close. Put that in the book. It will be an invitation."

"You're inviting people into a close relationship with you through something they read in a book?" I asked. "Don't you want to appear to them personally?"

"Personal invitations come in many formats," the king answered. "Are you ready to start working with me?"

"Yes, sir," I replied.

"Yes, we're ready to start," Salem affirmed. Excitement and confidence poured out of him. Most of his excitement wasn't over our working relationship. It was over the scores of people he'd begin working with soon. "Many people will work with me as a result of reading your book," he announced eagerly.

He looked me carefully in the eyes. "I judge you, Katharine. I judge you and proclaim you pure in heart. You're ready to work to restore heaven and earth."

FLAMING SWORD

"I believe you," I replied. "But I request the test of the Flaming Sword. I want it to judge the purity of my heart."

"There's no need for that, Katharine," Salem insisted. "My word is good enough around here. Besides, that sword will kill if it perceives corruption."

"I know. I don't doubt your judgment, king. But I want to form a foundation—a gateway—to enable creation to step into its purity. To do that, I request that the Flaming Sword be brought and subject my heart to its test. If I am completely pure, it will prove that corruption can be removed fully from all creation."

Nothing the king said could dissuade me. "People don't have to pass through that sword to enter the city," he urged.

But I insisted. Finally, the sword was brought to the palace gates. The crowd that had followed us up the hill regathered there. Anticipation surged through them.

When the Flaming Sword looked at me, it declared, "You may pass."

"That's not what I asked," I replied. "I don't want your permission to begin a journey towards never-ending life. I want you to judge me. I want everyone to know whether I am completely pure or not."

For some reason, the Flaming Sword didn't want to. I had to speak to it with my queenly authority, insisting it do as I bid.

With the King of Salem next to me and the inhabitants of his city watching in alarm, the Flaming Sword pierced my heart. Farther and farther into the depths of my heart, it plunged. The blade was wide and thin. The sensation of it sliding into my heart was pleasant. It felt smooth and quick.

"There is nothing impure in you," the sword declared as it removed its blade.

I turned with a knowing look to the king and the crowd. "Corruption can be erased from creation!" I declared. "I suspect that sword was crafted to cut the belief that we are impure from us. If the belief that we're corrupt is embedded deeply in us, then the sword may bring death before it brings life. But we can separate corruption—and the belief that we are corrupted—from us completely! It's time to build the new heaven and new earth from this understanding."

The crowd cheered in response. The king smiled softly. In his eyes, I could read how proud he was of me.

"I won't tolerate anyone even hinting that there could be something impure in any one of us, Salem," I whispered. "Don't let anyone who works with you suggest that's the case, either. Next time, I may call fire down to prove that there is not an ounce of corruption left in us."

"It's just the damn mindsets?" he asked, eyes twinkling.

"People die because of the mindsets we have about ourselves—not because of the reality of who we are," I agreed. "That's why we have to change how we see ourselves."

Chapter 23

The conference was in full swing when I returned to Salem's house. Most people were in afternoon lectures. A few lingered around tables displaying books set up in the hallways. Taking my time, I was winding down a main hall when Melchizedek hurried past. His robe was alive with electricity, floating inches off the ground as he moved swiftly by.

Noticing me, he paused. "I was looking for you," he barked. "Emergency. Yahweh demands your presence immediately. Follow me."

Resuming his brisk pace down the hall, he was soon well ahead of me. "What sort of emergency could happen in the King of Salem's house?" I wondered silently, jogging to catch up to him.

Melchizedek led us to a small, private office. I had been to Salem's larger office, where he held his one-on-one sessions. This smaller office was much more intimate. A fire was blazing in the fireplace near the doorway. But it took me several minutes to notice it because another fire was burning at his desk. The massive hard drive under his desk was on fire. I presumed that was the emergency.

"We have a situation," Yahweh announced.

Yahweh was dressed in regal clothes—a long, flowing, thick robe. Red and gold threads entwined in his clothing in a captivating way. Or maybe it was his face that was captivating. He was young, radiant, commanding, and altogether desirable.

"All the files for the conference are burning," he continued. "People believe you have something to do with this. You're being blamed, at least.

They also think you can fix it. We're at risk of losing everything discussed and unlocked here."

"Why is fire a problem?" I asked. "Isn't that a good thing? Won't everything released at this conference have been tested by fire? Its worth will be limitless now."

"Unless it all burns up," the King of Salem answered. I hadn't noticed him.

"I suspect this is the work of the Gate of Incorruptibility," I remarked. "It burns things that suggest that there's something wrong with you that needs to be fixed. My guess is that fire is burning through everything here, testing it. Anything religious will be consumed. Anything pure will remain. I wouldn't recommend putting that fire out."

"Perhaps she's right," Salem decided. "False alarm. We'll let this fire burn. It's worth the risk of losing every single teaching to prevent releasing something that wouldn't help humanity on the highest level possible."

"I agree," I voted. I wasn't sure if they were taking a vote or making an executive decision.

"Then that's what we'll do," Yahweh spoke. He seemed to be letting us decide how to handle the situation.

MELCHIZEDEK'S TRINITARIAN EXPRESSION

The emergency dealt with, the King of Salem turned to me. "I'm giving you these files—background information about me," he announced. He placed a massive stack of documents in my arms. "Review them. You need to know this about me to publish this book."

"Certainly," I agreed. I understood the imagery, too. The documents came from his *office*. So, they pertained to his *official* role. But they were filed in his *private* office. The information wasn't common knowledge.

Yahweh looked around the room, seeing if anyone had something to add.

"We're excited about this book," Melchizedek spoke up.

"It has our backing," the King of Salem agreed. "Our intention is for it to carry people into functioning at the highest levels—personally and for the world. We give our blessing to the book," he added, breathing on the stack of papers I held. "I'm opening your mind to understand me, Katharine, and to flow with me—so you can open the same understanding and flow for the world. You'll lay down everything else for a season so you can flow with me—and with all of this."

He leaned over me, breathing me in. With one hand, he gestured for Melchizedek to join him. Suddenly, the other two kings appeared next to him, too. Together, they encircled me. I felt their acceptance, their warmth, their affection. At the same time, they were doing something inside me.

"We're removing structures that would hinder what you need to release in this season of life," Salem explained. "And we're placing our signature on you."

Melchizedek stepped into me. Then, each king stepped into him. With all of them inside me, I realized something. Melchizedek is believed to be one of the original covering cherubs over the throne of Yahweh. (On the Old Testament ark, there were two cherubs that overshadowed Yahweh's throne. Those were images for the actual throne of God and the actual cherubs that overshadowed it.) From before the Beginning, Melchizedek was one of those cherubs. Lucifer was the other. Melchizedek observed Yahweh forming everything that exists through his breath, his words, his sound, his light.

It seemed fitting that Melchizedek—through the three kings that flowed from him—would be administering the formation of the new heaven and new earth. Melchizedek was an original witness to creation, understanding everything that was made and honoring all of Yahweh's plans. He knows the original design for everything. And his heart is turned towards Yahweh. He has both the knowledge and the love to administer the new heavens and new earth.

Melchizedek isn't a Son of God. But, as a reward for his heart towards Yahweh and creation, Melchizedek was "made like the Son of God" (Heb. 7:3 NKJV). Now, his role is as close as it gets to being a Son. He isn't creating like the Sons do. But he understands, administers, loves, and leads a process that is very similar to what he observed Yahweh doing in the Beginning.

It also made sense that we discovered the creation book here. Melchizedek wrote that book, we'd soon find out. The King of Salem— one of Melchizedek's expressions—guarded it. It was time for that book to be recovered because it was time for the new heaven and new earth to form. Melchizedek wanted humanity to do what we had been created to do. He wanted us to become fully like Yahweh—creators and sovereigns. After all these eons, his heart was still what it was before the Beginning: He loved Yahweh. Therefore, he loved us. He wanted us to flourish. And he'd do everything he could to help us along the way.

The administration of the Mountain couldn't have been given to anyone else. Melchizedek's trinitarian expression was the only logical choice. It was closing the loop on what had happened during creation. As a reward for how he responded to Yahweh's creation in the Beginning, Yahweh handed him administration of the new heavens and new earth.

When I understood those things, Melchizedek and the kings stepped out of me. But they didn't really leave me. Smiling broadly, we embraced.

In the group hug, I realized they had deposited something inside me that was attuned to their desires. I could sense what they wanted—what direction to turn in, what to open, what to close. Like how we can sense those things with Yahweh, I could now perceive their hearts.

Together, the kings anointed my head for the work I'd do with them. One by one, they whispered in my ear what their anointing carried.

"Write," the King of Peace whispered.

"Speak," said the King of Righteousness.

"Reveal," the King of Salem smiled.

Then they breathed into my core, and every worthy seed ever planted in my life came alive. Quickly, they grew into a beautiful garden. I knew their breath would flow through the words I'd later type to blow on every person reading this account.

Deeply moved, I touched each of them on the cheek briefly, looking them in the eye and thanking them. We breathed together a final time before they left the room in single file.

Chapter 24

That evening, the entire conference that the King of Salem had hosted at his house migrated to his city. Laughing, talking, and staring in wonder at the city, the throngs followed the path I had trekked up the streets to the palace. This time, no crowds gawked at them as they marched. They couldn't have, anyway. The troupe from the conference spilled over onto the sidewalks and alleys.

Some of the city's inhabitants stood on the upper level of their dwellings, waving handkerchiefs as the crowd filed past. Some cheered. The more enthusiastic ones threw confetti. A number of beings who lived or worked in the city joined the throng on their ascent. Worth, Glory, Holiness, and Splendor were among them.

I wasn't with the crowd. With the three kings, Melchizedek and some others, I stood on a balcony overlooking the path to the palace. "This is the best vantage point to write about the event, Katharine," Salem had explained when he asked me to join him there before the crowd migrated over.

The pre-party was no small thing, either. A live band played. Servants circulated with drinks and hors d'oeuvres. Scanning the balcony, I concluded the crowd here was mostly the conference speakers. I recognized a few people from earth. But my attention was drawn to a heavenly being. Excitedly, I hurried over to him.

IMMORTALITY

"Immortality!" I grinned. "I wondered why I hadn't seen you here earlier. Were you a conference speaker?"

"Absolutely," he replied.

Standing so close to him, I was overcome by how tall and muscular he looked. I hadn't remembered him being so large and strong. "Are you growing more powerful as more people align with you?" I asked.

"I believe so," he nodded excitedly. "I think I've grown three inches from this conference alone."

"Do you have anything to say for the book I'm writing?" I asked.

"People will have different journeys into immortality," he explained. "Some people will open it quickly. For others, it will be a slower process. Tell people not to be discouraged if others start after they do and finish before them. Once you're immortal, you're immortal. It doesn't matter when it happened. Many people's attitude about immortality will change in this next century or so," he continued. "Those changes will make it easier to access immortality. But don't wait for the changes to happen. If you want to access it now, then do. The door is open. That's one of the doors we're opening at this event."

"Oh, wow!" I exclaimed, honored to be part of it. "What other doors are opening?"

"A lot. Seeing far into the future in an insightful way is one door opening—I'm not sure what the term for that is," he answered. "We're laying the groundwork for abundance and prosperity to come in full force. Glory really wants to be released. I think she will be. But she'll come in a fuller measure later. Did I say Visions?"

"I don't think so."

"Visions, explanation of visions, insight, increase in whatever is already in someone's life," he rattled off quickly.

"A lot of things, then," I realized.

"Yes. These are the things I'm allowed to tell you for the book," Immortality grinned. "Basically, to those who have, much more will be given—until their cup is running over."

"I think you're combining two Bible verses."

Immortality shrugged. "And the people to whom the things are given will start to build amazing structures on earth—and in spiritual spaces. That's the reason things are being handed out. Artifacts, scrolls, and technologies that have been hushed for centuries are talking now. They've been silently waiting for this generation to arise. Now they're waking up because people are here who can do something with them. You're one of those people. So is everyone reading this book. My main message is to pick up your artifact, scroll, or technologically-empowered treasure. Then do what you're supposed to do with it."

I automatically reached for the pearls around my neck. Just then, the main gates of the palace opened, and the throng from the conference poured in. My conversation with Immortality ended abruptly as our attention turned to the festivities beginning inside.

DINNER

Tonight, I was seated in the middle of the King of Salem's table. On either side of me were people I didn't recognize. Paul sat directly across from me tonight. I hadn't seen Don all evening. I spent most of dinner chatting with the 12th-century monk to my right. He kept me on the edge of my seat with his fascinating stories. I longed to talk to Paul in a quieter setting. I had questions that he'd be the perfect person to ask. I even suspected he had asked to sit near me to share his insights. But dinner didn't provide that opportunity. Perhaps afterward, I thought.

Immediately after dessert was served, though, someone leaned over my shoulder from behind.

"We need to talk," Don spoke quietly but firmly.

He had an intense, no-nonsense, work-mode expression on his face.

His eyes burned with the kind of fire that gets things done by consuming anything in its way. I wasn't sure yet what he thought was in his way. But I certainly didn't want to have anything to do with it.

"Of course," I replied. Hurriedly, I excused myself from the table, smiling at Paul in a way that I hoped let him know I'd love to chat later.

All business, Don whisked me past the ballrooms where people danced for fun or deeper connection or oneness. In those rooms, people were bonding with others in those ways in their dances. It seemed to be an incredible way to end three days of being together. But Don had a different agenda. Determinedly, he led us to a small sitting area next to the ballroom designed for alignment. Now, his intentions were clear. He wanted us to align more fully so we could work together with no hindrances. Elegant chairs interspersed with small tables provided a view of the dance floor—or a place to rest between dances. Choosing seats closest to the dancing, he motioned for me to sit down.

ALIGNING

The music in that ballroom was releasing frequencies that helped the dancers align with each other. Purposefully, Don had positioned us near those frequencies. We sat silently for several minutes, taking in the music as we watched the couples dancing. Tonight, everyone wore the same style of clothes as the three kings and Melchizedek. So all the men wore colorful suits spun from thick, royal thread. The suits extended to their mid-thighs. Buttons made of gold lined the jackets down the middle. The woman wore floor-length gowns spun from the same royal thread. Most gowns were lined with crinolines under the skirts, reminding me of ancient queens in their full regalia.

After several minutes, Don broke the silence. "You believe our alignment is off," he stated.

"It's not totally off."

"I want to answer your questions, Katharine, not bite your head off."

"It may be easier if you just bit my head off," I smiled. "It's my mind that has the problems, not my spirit."

"I know," he answered gently. "I realize you've recently changed a lot of your beliefs to step into these things. Stop thinking it's 'good' to change your beliefs for one reason and 'bad' to change your beliefs for another reason. Your ability to radically change your beliefs—for whatever reason—will keep you at the cutting edge. Revelation is always expanding. When people don't expand with it, they get stuck in old seasons. Embrace the changes you've made. It's what's enabling you to move into greater and greater levels of glory."

"Remember the day I took everything I had gained spiritually and laid it at your feet—in response to what Yahweh showed me about you? I died, in a sense, when I did that," I told him. "You knew it. Do you remember what you said to me?"

"No greater love has anyone than this—to lay down one's life for one's friend," Don remembered.

"Yes, except we were barely even friends," I chuckled. "If I died then, I've continued to die every day. Sometimes, it feels like I am laying my life down for this constantly."

"What do you mean?" Don asked, concerned.

"I had what I thought were amazing revelations that Yahweh had given me for humanity," I explained. "Most of my revelations are the same as yours, of course. But some peripheral ideas weren't. I've laid those down. I've gone against what my mind believed to be a higher truth. It feels like dying to what I thought I'd do. I constantly swallow my pride. A voice whispers that I'm not being true to myself or what Yahweh gave me to release on the earth."

"I'm assuming there's a 'but' in here somewhere," Don prompted when I stopped speaking.

"But every time I look at you, I feel your worth. I know that who you are and what you will release to the universe is far greater than anything

I know currently. If my revelation disagrees with your revelation, then I trust your revelation," I answered. "So I die to myself every day. I—"

"We're going to take care of this right here, right now," Don spoke like someone taking control over a crisis and restoring order. "Years from now, people will ask you why you changed your beliefs. I'll show you the answer I want you to give them."

Pausing to ensure he had my attention, he said, "I want you to see what your future would look like two ways. First, look at your life if you didn't die to the revelation Yahweh entrusted you with. Then, look at your life if you lay down that revelation and flow with my revelation. Look deeply and be sure."

As he spoke, a portal opened in my spiritual vision. For several minutes, I peered into it. I saw two paths emerge for my life and how things would unfold both ways.

"I can't see specifics of what would happen," I finally announced. "But I can tell that it goes much better for me if I'm willing to lay down my revelation and embrace yours. It's not even close. The best possible path for my life opens when I align fully with you."

Don smiled.

"But I didn't lay my life down for a higher revelation, Don. I think you realize that. No matter how amazing, a revelation isn't worth dying for. Yeshua said he laid his life down for his *friends*, not for a new theology he brought. Only other people are worthy of our greatest sacrifices. When we see a person who so thoroughly reflects Yahweh's image that all of creation will be transformed by the revelation that flows from him— that's what's worthy of laying everything down for."

Don was silent for a moment, letting my words sink in. "You know that someone who gives a glass of water to a man or woman of God— because of who they are—will be rewarded," Don finally spoke, referring to Matthew 10:41–42. "Can you imagine how tremendous your reward will be for laying down everything for someone in response to who they are?"

"I hadn't looked at it like that," I answered.

"Start seeing what will open to you as a result of the choices you've made. Don't think about what you're giving up. Think about what you're gaining," Don counseled. "I want to give you one more way to look at what's happening. Yeshua said, 'unless a kernel of wheat falls to the ground and dies, it remains only a single seed. But if it dies, it produces many seeds. Anyone who loves their life will lose it, while anyone who hates their life in this world will keep it for eternal life' (John 12:24-25 NIV). Choosing to die every day is the only way to get what you're after. Because you've died to your old ways of thinking—because you've hated your life in this world—you will open eternal life inside you—and inside many others."

"I had thought only about how difficult it was to die to myself every day," I answered. "I hadn't realized that was the path into eternal life and everything else I've always wanted."

"It is. If you had chosen any other path, life may be temporarily easier. But you'd never unlock what your heart desires," he answered. He paused to give me time to process what he'd said. "So, are we good now?"

"We're good," I sighed as peace overwhelmed me.

"Then I'm going to get a drink," Don announced. "Would you like anything?"

"Bring me whatever you're having. I'm living by Solomon's motto this weekend."

"Eat, drink, and be merry?" Don grinned as he headed to the bar.

PAUL

I was fidgeting with my dress when a man approached me.

"Is now a good time?" he smiled.

"Paul! I'm so glad to see you. Yes, now is great."

As he settled into the chair Don had been sitting in, I thought about how wonderful it was to see him again. I was eager to jump into a conversation. But he wanted to connect spiritually first. "Align yourself with me more closely so I can share things with you on a deeper level," he urged.

So we sat on the edge of the dance floor, aligning for several minutes.

"Want to dance?" he finally asked. I think he wanted to take the alignment deeper. "This is the ballroom for aligning, isn't it?"

"Yes, and yes," I laughed, taking his hand as he led us to the dance floor.

For several minutes, we twirled around the dance floor as we touched the part of each other that could explain mysteries and new theological concepts. He was unlocking that place inside me, charging it up.

"Your greatest theological writings lie ahead of you," he told me. "Don't worry about leaving behind anything you've written so far. That was your warm-up."

I laughed.

He spent several minutes encouraging me, like he had in the past, to boldly leave behind outdated theology. "Don't be afraid to push beyond what I saw," he counseled. "That's what I would do if I lived now."

"That's what you did in your day," I smiled. "You left behind the religion you grew up with. I feel like I'm doing the same thing."

"You are. So do it boldly," he urged. "I see some old theology still in you. Mind if I fish it out?"

"Go ahead," I laughed.

"Not many people would do what you're doing, Katharine. But I applaud you for it."

"I feel compelled to do what I'm doing. I think you felt the same way about leaving traditional Judaism."

He laughed. "Yes, a good way of putting it."

"I find it fascinating that the people who criticize the new beliefs that we're talking about at this conference hold you in such esteem," I told Paul, smiling. "They applaud you for being considered a heretic and for being kicked out of synagogues to champion a fuller understanding of Yahweh. Yet those same people call us heretics. They kick us out of their circles. It seems they're treating us how the Jews treated you. I'm not criticizing them. I think they're right for doing it—just like it was right to call you a heretic and kick you out of synagogues. We do have different beliefs. They each need their own space to thrive in. I just find it interesting."

"I'm glad the suffering I went through to bring a higher revelation can be an encouragement to you, Katharine," Paul replied.

Paul danced with me for a long time, inspiring me to live at my highest potential with thoughtful advice. Right before he left, he said, "You smell like wildflowers tonight."

"That's not my normal scent. Are you saying I'm wild?"

"No, I'm saying your fragrance will be delightful, wildly delightful, to many—no matter where you write your theology from. Goodnight."

CHANGE

I wandered off the dance floor, nearly colliding with several couples. The conversation with Paul left me deep in thought.

"Earth to Katharine," Don smiled. "Or I should say Heaven to Katharine. Your chair—and perhaps more importantly, your drink—is over here."

Don was seated in the same place, two drinks resting on the table beside him.

"Have you ever felt that everything in your life is about to turn upside down? And you're not sure if you should be super happy about it or terribly sad?" I asked him as I took my seat.

"I've found it's better to face change head-on than try to resist it," Don replied. "Change is coming for far more than just your life. It will sweep through the whole world. Those who position themselves to embrace the change will move higher, faster."

"That's good advice," I sighed.

"Everything's going to turn out better than you're imagining."

"Really? Because I can imagine pretty big, Mr. Joseph," I brightened. "I can imagine living on earth for tens of thousands of years, blessing my generational line as I unlock the things for humanity we've always longed for. I can imagine myself becoming fully sovereign, flowing in all knowledge and all power as I'm everywhere all at once."

"I can do more than *imagine* big," Don grinned. "Look down the timeline and see what's coming. Don't look just at your life. Look at the whole earth."

I took a moment to do as he suggested. Soon, I was hit with the feeling of what lay ahead. How would you feel if you possessed everything your heart had yearned for? What would be worth giving up or going through to get it? My mood turned from deep contemplation to overwhelming joy and excitement.

"No wonder the Bible says every tear is wiped away," I smiled, thinking of Revelation 21:4. "Seeing what lies ahead—what we're opening now—is enough to turn any sadness into ecstasy."

"It's an honor to be alive in this day," Don told me solemnly. "The day it all began."

Chapter 25

The crowds flocked from the city back to the house. It was the last night there. I decided to make the most of it. Rummaging through the nightgowns in Salem's closet, I found the most queenly-looking one. It was sewn of the same thick, costly thread that the three kings wore. Mostly deep blue, the gown had gold and red intermingled in it. The nightgown itself was form-fitting and sleeveless. But its matching robe had long sleeves that flared at the end. With the robe tied around my waist, I looked ready to go to a royal banquet, not to bed.

As I slipped into bed, I grabbed the book on engravings that I had borrowed from Salem's library. I hadn't made much progress on it. Two minutes into my studies, I was interrupted again. A golden, translucent being appeared in the middle of the room.

"The King of Salem summons you to his private chambers," she announced. "You may follow me through the secret passages."

Intrigued, I wrapped my robe around my waist and scurried towards the wall panel that had slid open.

We wove through the house's hidden passageways. As we were navigating, the king began talking to me. I could see myself in his chambers and also traveling to his chambers. I knew he was showing me that we already had a close relationship, and we were also on our way to forming a close relationship. Eventually, the translucent being opened a door and motioned for me to step inside.

FIRESIDE CHAT

I was in his private quarters. They were decorated in the same elegant style as the rest of the house—except with more gold. A floor-length mirror, trimmed ornately in gold, was the first thing that caught my eye. Then I noticed all the furniture was bordered with gold. Bookcases lined one wall. Opulent sofas and chairs were arranged near a fireplace. Through an open door, I could see an elegant bed in what must have been his bedroom. We were in the sitting area of his private chambers.

"Join me by the fire, Katharine," the king called. "I've placed our drinks on the table there."

We both sat on the sofa that faced the cracking fire. Salem was wearing informal clothes. They looked costly and regal. But they were mostly plain white. His robe, however, was bordered with elegant deep blue embroidering, almost the same color as my outfit. He had left his sash unfastened. It dangled on either side of him, giving our conversation a more casual feel.

"Tell me about yourself, Katharine," the king began.

"What do you want to know?" I asked.

"Everything."

I laughed. "That may take two interviews," I smiled. "There's not much to know. I grew up in a very loving, very conservative Christian home." I rose, walking to the edge of the fireplace before continuing. Staring into the fire, I told him, "My family thinks I'm a heretic for talking to spirits like yours. They think if you talk to any spirit but God's, you're interacting with a demon."

"Yet you continue to interact in the realms with spirits like mine," Salem noted.

"Of course I do," I quipped. Turning to face him, I explained. "I see who you are. I know what you can open to humanity. People in past generations made the choices they did about how to live their spiritual lives. What did it get them? Death. If I make the choices they did, why should I expect a different outcome? I'm choosing life, Salem. I'm choosing to unlock my divine nature. And I don't care who calls me a heretic for doing so."

"You have a boldness that I like, Katharine," the king replied. "I want to work with you."

"I already signed the contract you offered me," I exhaled, joining him on the sofa again.

"I want more than that contract. I want our houses to align," Salem announced. "I'm making a formal offer to you now to align our houses."

"You want my daughter to marry your son?" I joked.

"I like how you think, Katharine," Salem chuckled. "Not that kind of alliance. An alignment between me and you." When I didn't immediately respond, he added, "Think about it. My offer remains open. In the meantime, all this is yours. I open my house to you. You're welcome to come anytime. I also open my heart to you, Katharine. And I don't do that with nearly as many people."

I laughed.

"You hold something important for humanity. And I'm determined to bring it out of you," Salem continued.

"And I'd like to take the important gift you have for humanity and help you present that to the world," I smiled.

ALIGNMENT

Later, I returned to the encounter to give him my well-thought-out answer. "I'm ready to align our houses," I announced.

"Good, I was hoping you'd say that," Salem grinned. Eagerly, he motioned for me to join him by the fire.

We stood in front of the fire, staring into its hungry flames. He wanted us to jump in. I could feel it inside him.

"We're going to align through fire," he told me.

After initially protesting, I summoned courage and jumped into the fire with him. We stood in its bright flames, facing each other, letting the flames hunt in every inch of our beings.

"I want you to say this with me, Katharine, 'Anything in me that doesn't line up with our purposes together, I let the fire consume.'"

"That seems pretty extreme," I protested. The flames were so loud I was nearly shouting. "What if there's something wonderful that doesn't fit with our purposes together but fits with something else?"

Maybe it was the lawyer in me, maybe it was the skeptic, but I wanted a re-write. I proposed that the intention be to burn anything that didn't fit with the highest purposes for my life. In the end, though, I looked the King of Salem in the eyes, fire burning around us, and intended for any scroll in my life that didn't line up with his house to be burned.

"You're not going to burn all my scrolls, will you?" I asked.

"I'd never burn the ones you're worried about, Katharine. They lie at the core of who you are," the king assured me.

I did see scrolls—assignments heaven had released to me—burning in the fire. One project in particular came to mind. It was a book I had written (but not published). Salem wanted it burned. That scroll had been handed to me by an archangel. I thought it held the potential to shift humanity. I wrote it with a pretty heavy anointing. For weeks the year before, I had poured my heart into it. But staring into Salem's eyes, I realized it was a "lesser" scroll for my life. Yes, it could change the world. But it would conflict with how Salem wanted to change the world with me. And what he desired was far, far better. So I let the fire burn it. The next morning on earth, I erased the files from my computer—crying as I did so.

Other scrolls burned in the fire with Salem, too. I wasn't consciously aware of what they were. But I knew this was the first step of working together—aligning my mission with his. Salem was doing the same thing with me, too. He was opening up his life, letting the fire burn anything that didn't align with our purposes together. It was a two-way street.

Later, I remembered when the King of Salem's computer hard drive was on fire, and I was blamed for it. Was he letting fire burn through his computer files as I had purged mine? Had the fire consumed anything that his house could release that was a lesser revelation than what I had unlocked?

ASHES

Burnt scrolls didn't mean wasted time, I discovered. The fire didn't destroy. It transmuted. Those projects may be ashes. But Yahweh explained to me once that the ashes of something burned with fire are more valuable than the most beautiful project that hasn't been passed through fire. The ashes of those projects could be traded for something far greater than what the projects themselves would have released.

I used to think that only worthless things were consumed by fire. Now I realized that wasn't true. I couldn't call the scrolls handed to me by archangels or Yahweh himself worthless. I was setting the caliber for my life so high now that even those kinds of projects would burn. I wanted my highest purposes—and only my highest—released. Why spend time on anything less? So, some wonderful things burned in my life. Perhaps they were doing the same in Salem's.

CITY

After the fire burned my exterior, it penetrated straight to my core. There, it didn't consume the scrolls. It turned them into gold. As the fire burned longer, the gold liquified and spilled down my insides—opening the depths of who I am.

When I saw what lay inside my core, I was shocked. "Salem, it's a city!" I shouted. "I am a city."

His eyes sparkled in delight for me. I remembered something Don told me once. When Jesus said, "A city set on a hill cannot be hidden,"

(Matt. 5:14 ESV), he was talking about us, Don explained. We are a city. And we're meant to shine our light. These events at the King of Salem's house were about his city. But each of us was a city, too. The world needed all of our cities released.

TEST

"Come with me," Salem beckoned. Quickly, he grabbed my hand and hopped out of the fire.

When we emerged from the fire, our outfits had transformed. Instead of casual clothes, we were wearing gowns worthy of when kings and queens sit on thrones. Gold crowns studded with jewels rested on our heads. Our skin was sparkling. Minuscule, dazzling gemstones were radiating out of our bodies. He held one of my hands lightly in his, our fingers entwined. We were staring each other in the eyes. If this was a visual representation of what aligning houses meant, then whatever we had done was stunning.

"You did it, Katharine," Salem beamed. "You passed the test."

"The fire was a test?" I laughed.

"It sure was. Were you going to pass all of yourself through the fire? Or would you withhold some? Most people tend to withhold some parts. To the mind, that seems like the most reasonable thing to do. But you gave all of yourself to the flames. It cost you now. But there will be a huge payoff in the years ahead. Whatever people keep back from the fire will pull at them, bringing them off course down the road."

"How do you know if you've given all of yourself or withheld something?" I wondered.

"Most people don't know. They think they've given it all. But you asked the flames to burn all of you. You pointed out the parts you didn't think had been reached, asking the fire to touch you there," Salem remarked.

"Being criticized helps," I told him. "I've been very criticized by people close to me recently. I feel like they find fault with everything about me. Their constant commentary makes me want to pass all of myself through the fire—just to prove to myself that I've tested everything about me— and it's all okay!" I laughed. "I'm so thankful for the criticism. It's pushing me to throw out anything less than the best thing for my life."

"I can tell. That's often why heaven orders criticism as part of people's diet," Salem told me.

I laughed again. "I want to start. Let's get to the substance of what we'll do together."

"I like that, Katharine. I want that, too. Why don't we start with syncing our hearts? I want to do this right, set a firm foundation," Salem explained.

"Yes, of course," I nodded.

HEART SYNC

We stood facing each other. Then we looked into each other's eyes with the intent of getting to know the other person. It always amazes me how much better you can get to know someone in heaven doing that. I could feel his motivations behind what he did. I knew what animated him was the highest virtues. It felt like he was showing me different rooms inside him. Instead of giving me a tour of his "physical" house, he gave me a tour of himself. He let me taste, sample, and enjoy.

After we had synced our hearts for several minutes, Salem said, "Wait right there. I want to serve you my wine."

When he returned, he was carrying two glasses of wine. And soft music was playing in the background.

As he fiddled with the fire, I sampled his wine. It was remarkably rich. "This is the best wine I've ever tasted!" I exclaimed. "I'm impressed, Salem."

He grinned, clearly pleased. "That's from my private vineyard. I have wine from a public vineyard and wine from a private one. I'm serving you the private vintage. I do that when I want people to get to know me personally, not just professionally."

"That makes sense," I nodded.

"Sit with me by the fire," he beckoned, moving chairs extremely close to the hearth. In the background, the music sang a soft, slow melody. "I want to sync more than our hearts," he explained. "Let's synch our movements, our rhythms, our patterns. Flow with me," he instructed.

From deep inside him, I could hear him releasing a sound. Visually, it looked like a guitar string running through his core was being plucked. When I heard the frequency, I echoed it back to him.

"We're entraining our frequencies," Salem smiled. "I'm doing the same with you. You're releasing your sound and I'm humming until I align with that." After thirty or sixty minutes, he announced, "I've just taken you through the equivalent of spending one earth year entraining to my frequency. We've stepped outside of time to do that. Listen now. You respond to even the slightest moves of my spirit, right?"

He sounded what looked like a short, small guitar string inside his core. Instantly, my spirit echoed it back.

"That's all the entraining we need," he told me. "But I'm going to keep you here because I can."

For a while longer, we flowed together—in and out of time. He'd take us to a realm where time didn't exist—and then back into a realm with time. I'm not sure how long we did that. I'm not sure it's possible to tell.

LIFE CHANGING

"From the first moment you spoke to me, I knew you'd change my life forever," I confided as the wine opened my heart to him.

"Was it that dramatic?" he grinned.

"Far more so. When you asked me to work with you, I instantly realized we could do something important together. But I'd have to leave my path and move onto your path to do it. I decided right then and there

I'd leave everything to work with you. You're worthy of leaving what I was doing before I met you."

"And you are worthy of everything I am laid at your feet," he replied.

"Is that what you're doing now? Dumping who you are before me?" I smiled. His insides were open and vulnerable to me.

"I'm doing far more than that, Katharine. When you left everything for me, it opened a possibility between us—one we can both benefit from. I'm trading into that possibility being opened to its fullest potential."

Gemstones fell from his person onto the floor at my feet. "I'm trading, Katharine, so you'll open more of yourself to me."

THREE KEYS

On earth, we spent hours together. I went about my life on earth as usual. But I was also aware of being with the King of Salem by the fire in his private chambers.

Eventually, he reached into his pocket and removed three keys linked on a chain. With a ceremonious look on his face, he handed them to me.

"The first key is to the collection of my private vintage wine. You may open a personal relationship with me to others," he explained. "It's completely your discretion who you serve the wine to." Leaning in, he whispered, "But start with Don."

"I thought Don had the keys to everything in your house—" I began. Then I decided not to question him. "Of course."

"The second key is to the 13th Mountain," Salem continued.

"Thank you, but I already have a key to the mountain."

"This is my personal key. It opens for you anything that I have access to," he clarified. "Use it well."

"And the third key?" I prompted when he grew silent.

"That is the key to my heart," Salem replied, averting his eyes. "It is the most powerful of the three."

I smiled. "Yes, I believe you. That's how it worked with Yahweh, too." When I placed the keys on the buckle around my waist, something shifted. "What just happened?" I asked the king, slightly alarmed. "Something shifted when I accepted your keys. I took an official position in relation to your house, didn't I? What changed between us?" I pressed.

"Everything," he whispered.

EVEN BETTER

"You want to get started on the substance of what we'll do together," he told me a moment later. "You wonder why I'm spending all this time building our connection first. Sit in the mystery of what I'm doing, Katharine. Dwell on it. Don't move on until you've figured it out."

Eventually, I realized that he was the key to what we'd do together. It wasn't his wisdom or his access or his knowledge. It was him.

"I am a gateway into everything in the Mountain," he explained. "So I'm a gateway into everything you seek to build through any blueprint you take from that Mountain. You can step into me and build it." Looking me in the eye, he declared forcefully, "Through me, you will have a series of encounters in Eden. Write them in a book. Those encounters will help open Eden to humanity again. You'll discover that—"

"The new heaven and new earth must be built from Eden's perspective," I finished his thought. "We'll literally return to the original design and build from there. We can't form perfection from here. We must see that design, live in it, touch it, have it flow through us in order to build it."

"Yes, you'll discover it's more complicated and beautiful. But, yes, you're right," Salem smiled. He breathed powerfully onto me. "The encounters will begin right away. But stay with me here awhile, too. I open up awareness of multiple dimensions simultaneously to you."

So I stayed with him in his private chambers, flowing with him in a sweet connection. And I also went to Eden—and had an amazing opening encounter for that book. Later, I thought about the book I erased from my computer. It, too, was about Eden. Was the King of Salem opening to me a book that would have a far greater impact than the one I had burned for him?

In his chamber, the king whispered, "I have some things I want to tell you, but not in this book."

"Understood," I nodded.

"So you're dismissed," he announced, gesturing towards the secret panel, still swung open. I raised my eyebrows at him. After connecting so deeply for so long, he could dismiss me with the brush of his hand? I guess he could. Quickly, I hurried towards the exit.

Chapter 26

The translucent being who had guided me to Salem's room wasn't dispatched to pilot me back. I guess Salem assumed I had memorized the route. I'm not sure if I made a wrong turn or if I forgot to walk down to my floor. When I opened the door I thought would land me in my room, I found myself in the most colossal guest bedroom suite I had ever seen. Ten times larger than mine, the suite had an elegant fireplace (with a roaring fire), a generous sitting room, and built-in bookcases lining almost every wall. I was about to close the door when a familiar voice called my name.

"Katharine, what an unusual way to pay someone a visit."

So this was Don's palatial quarters.

"They give the speakers much larger rooms than the people writing books," I told him, peeking through the doorway. "This is gorgeous."

"Come in," Don beckoned. "Can you stay? I invited Moshe for a visit. I'm sure he'd love to see you."

"I'd love to see him," I brightened, stepping fully into the room. "But I don't want to intrude."

"I'm pretty sure entering someone's room uninvited through a secret passage is the definition of intruding," Don grinned. "But you're not intruding in the sense you mean. I was just pouring drinks. I'll pour a third for you."

MOSHE

Just then, there was a knock on the door. When Moshe entered, he didn't seem surprised to see me. Grabbing both my arms with his hands, he pulled me towards him and kissed me heartily on the cheek. "It's good to see you in person," he beamed.

"I'm pretty sure this is still a vision," I winked. "But it does feel more life-like."

Ushering us to the sitting area, Don urged us to join him around the coffee table. Moshe took the sofa. Don and I sat in chairs opposite each other.

"So, what did you want to talk about tonight?" Moshe asked.

I hoped Don wanted to discuss the terrifyingly amazing book we had discovered. When I glanced at Don, I noticed he had placed the book on the table. We had the same thought.

"What do you want to tell us about this book?" Don asked.

"That book was one of my greatest treasures for a season," Moshe began.

"If it was a great treasure for you, how did it end up in a dusty attic?" I wondered.

"What is a treasure during one season of life can become something holding you back in another season," Moshe replied. "That book helped me understand creation deeply. But then, I needed to move on to explore other things. If we hold onto treasures from past seasons, we don't have room to grasp the new wonders that want to open to us."

Moshe paused to look and Don and me carefully, emphasizing the weight of his words. Then he continued. "I've been safeguarding what's in that book. You may think it wasn't guarded because it was lying in a dusty room. But it was kept in a hidden attic in Salem's house, guarded by my spiders and their fierce webs. And it was locked in a room to which few have the keys. Vaults come in all shapes and sizes.

"The book was written by Melchizedek," Moshe continued, shifting his weight slightly as he spoke. "He captured the sound of creation. One day, he wanted to be able to discuss those mysteries with us—the ones he foresaw Yahweh creating in his image. The book was a technology to preserve those moments so we could have full access to it later. Melchizedek is the one who entrusted the book to me."

"That's why the book was in the King of Salem's attic," I realized. "Salem came from Melchizedek. So it would make sense that you gave it to him for safekeeping later."

"There were three copies of that book made," Moshe continued. "You now possess one of them."

CREATION'S MYSTERIES

"What's the book about?" Don cut to the chase.

"The book contains an understanding of creation," Moshe continued. "I'm ready to pass on an understanding of creation to others. By giving you that book, I am signifying that I'm handing a deep, unprecedented understanding of how creation happened to select others—as well as how the creation process itself works."

"You're passing on a historical understanding of what happened when Yahweh created? And you're handing off an understanding of the general principles used when creating?" I asked for clarity.

"Yes, both of those aspects of creation," Moshe nodded. "They're both in that book. Understanding creation is one of many things I've been safeguarding. By passing it on to others, I will be free to pursue other things I've wanted to explore. Those things will be crucial for what's coming, too."

"Why are you passing it on now?" I asked.

"Because there is a new generation arising on the earth—unlike any generation before them," Moshe answered. "They are so different that I think of them like a new breed of people. When this new breed interacts with ancient wisdom, they can digest it in ways prior generations couldn't. They read texts with the wisdom of the ancients. Then, they execute what they read with the intelligence accumulated through generations of human existence. In short, they will be able to do things with these texts that no other humans have ever done."

Pausing to make eye contact with us both, Moshe announced, "You are from this new breed." Laying his fingers on the book, he said, "Go, do with it more than what I did, than anyone before you did. Make it your own."

I looked from Moshe to Don. Moshe's words inspired me. But the terror I felt when I opened the book still rang inside me. Don smiled at me reassuringly. His eyes seemed to say, "We can do this. Be courageous."

SAFEKEEPING

"One more thing. And this is important. I'm not passing on just the knowledge in the book. I'm passing on the safekeeping of that knowledge. Guard the book. Put it somewhere safe. Perhaps in Don's house. You'll know what you need to keep the book secure. It's not something to be floating around in the universe, unattended."

He didn't need to tell us why. We had the experience to prove that the book's power was both dangerous and life-giving.

"But this is all happening in the context of a book I'm writing," I objected. "I'm not sure if we'll ever publish this book. But if we do, are we making the creation book vulnerable?"

"You'll know what to do. And so will the creation book. You can ask it what it wants to do to stay safe. There are many options," Moshe answered.

"Let's put a lock on the book," I suggested to Don. "That way, everyone can see that the book exists. They can receive an invitation to open its contents. But its mysteries will unlock only to those who have the key."

"You know locks don't stop someone like me," Don replied. "I could

2

jump into the contents of that book even if you put a thousand locks on it."

"Nothing is hidden from you, Don. You've reached that level. 'Nothing in all creation is hidden from God's sight. Everything is uncovered and laid bare before the eyes of him to whom we must give account' (Heb. 4:13 NIV). When someone is ready to judge, then the record of everything is open to them. I'm not worried about people like you reading this book. But for those not ready for its contents, it's dangerous. Locks child-proof things. They never keep adults out."

"May I speak?" the book asked. To my surprise, it spoke in a stunning masculine voice. Yet wisps of feminine beauty trailed behind its sound.

"Of course," the three of us echoed.

"I've been hidden from the Beginning, used only by a select few. I'm happy to come out and share my secrets. But I'm not ready to share them broadly now. Don't put a lock around me. Put me in a vault. Make me seen only to those who can find me."

Immediately, Don rose and placed the book in a wall safe in his guest quarters. "We'll keep the book locked up. No one can access it unless they have the keys to my safe."

Locked in Don's vault, the book would be far more than childproofed. Even mature, wise adults couldn't access it without his express permission.

"You know what you just did, Don?" I asked amazingly. "You just became the guardian of the book Moshe guarded for millennia. It's officially in your hands now."

"It's a bit in your hands, too, Katharine," he winked. "We're safeguarding this together."

"By placing it in your vault," I laughed. "My point remains."

JEWELRY

The safeguarding of the book settled, Don turned to a related topic. "What do you know about jewelry related to the book?" he asked Moshe.

"I'm not aware that any jewelry was crafted from that book," Moshe answered. "But sometimes, artifacts have jewelry forged from their essence. Jewelry enables what the artifact contains to be displayed or carried into other contexts."

"Can jewelry help people use the artifact better?" I wondered.

"Certainly," Moshe replied. "Jewelry can speak to you about the same sort of things the artifact would. It carries its essence. So, wearing the jewelry is like carrying the artifact in your heart. You have it on you, speaking to you constantly about its nature."

Don left the sitting area momentarily to retrieve his pearl cufflinks. Handing them to Moshe, he asked, "What do you think about these?"

"Wow," Moses whistled. "These little cufflinks are talkative. Both the gold and the pearl are talking."

"Yes," I laughed. "His cufflinks are very chatty."

"When jewelry is talkative, that means it wants to open its mysteries to you fully," Moshe explained. "It's gearing up to spill everything it knows into you."

"So the contents of the creation book want to open fully to Don now?" I asked for clarity.

"Yes, certainly," Moshe nodded.

"My pearls aren't as talkative," I realized.

"Not yet, but they're shining brilliantly, aren't they?" Moshe asked. "When they shine, they're pouring illumination into your heart, preparing the way for their voice to be released to you."

BLESSING

"I want to bless both of you as you take a leadership role in these topics," Moshe announced.

Walking to the fireplace, he motioned for us to join him. The fire was blazing strongly. Its yellow and orange flames seemed to be competing to soar higher into the darkness of the flue. Moshe turned towards the fire, opening himself to its flames.

"It's time," he spoke in a grave tone. "The mysteries that have been hidden in darkness are being revealed. You two will be on the cutting edge of their revelation. So will everyone at this conference—if they choose to pursue it."

Don and I were standing behind Moshe, looking at the fire. Turning around to face us, Moshe placed a hand on both of our cheeks. He took turns looking us in the eye. His gaze penetrated me to the core. It felt like he was peering into my deepest places, observing things I wasn't aware of myself. Without words, he invited me to do the same. My being entered his space—searching, finding, celebrating, holding.

As we continued exchanging, I noticed that the three of us were standing in a circle. Information and power circled counter-clockwise among us, gently building in intensity.

One goal Moshe had, it seemed, was for us to get to know him better. Instead of chatting for hours to tell us about himself as someone would do on earth, he flashed images of his childhood, his adult years, major turning points, and fun moments into our minds. He didn't need to explain the significance of each memory because he transmitted what he was feeling at the time. And he transmitted how he processed it later—how the moment impacted him.

As a result, I came to know Moshe much better. A oneness was forming. It wasn't the full oneness that he longed for, that people from heaven enjoyed with each other. But it was a far deeper connection than a casual chat with someone in the cloud of witnesses creates.

Then Moshe transmitted images about what he wanted to do with us. He also conveyed his feelings about us personally—warm affection bubbling with joy. Working with him would generate pure ecstasy among us. I hadn't realized that *working* could create such a high.

The longer we exchanged, the more intense it became. Fire encircled my heart. Tingling bliss raced down my arms and legs. Power shot out of my feet. Meanwhile, passageways were forming inside each of us for deeper exchanges as we worked together.

There were many important things about that late-night chat with Moshe—understanding the creation book and having mysteries handed off to us. But I could tell the most valuable part of the evening, at least from Moshe's point of view, was the connection he was forming with us.

Chapter 27

I bid the men a good night. But they insisted on walking me to my room—through the public hallways. They didn't want to risk my getting lost again.

When we were standing in front of my door, Don asked me, "What was the most important part of this book for you?"

The book was drawing to a close, I realized. We had a few hours left in Salem's house. Then, everyone would go their separate ways. I reflected on all the things we had done over the last three days: The terrifyingly wonderful encounter in the attic, the chats with amazing people from heaven, the time with Salem himself, and the worth of everything in this place.

"The most wonderful thing was the excitement," I decided. "Being here made me feel like something heart-stoppingly wonderful is about to happen. I feel like my wildest dreams are going to come true. Something is coming on earth and in my life that will be worth every hardship, every sacrifice, every ounce of effort to birth it. We're standing on the brink of what everyone who's ever lived has wanted to see. And we get to see it. We get to bring it to life."

"I know," he replied, awe in his voice. "It's incredible."

The three of us stood silently in the hall as excitement bubbled inside us. Soon, our excitement was bouncing off each other, growing in intensity.

"Don't turn in quite yet," Moshe told us. "There are a few of us gathering on the rooftop patio. Join us. We hadn't intended to invite anyone on earth. But I think you both should be there."

"I'm in," Don and I said simultaneously.

"Follow me, then," Moshe called over his shoulder. He was already part-way down the hall. "We'll watch things unfold from the highest point around."

LAST PARTY

A party was in progress in a room not far from the secret attic we had explored our first night. Sliding glass doors lined an entire wall, revealing a sky full of stars. Salem had arranged elegant chairs and comfortable sofas to provide a stunning view of the night sky. The sliding doors were all pulled open to give access to a spacious balcony. Outside, patio furniture was positioned so small groups could gather outdoors and enjoy the view from the roof.

From there, you could see the other dimensional beings coming and going as they brought things for the earth. You could observe people from heaven as they arrived or left. You could watch the earth's response to everything. In hushed tones, small groups were commenting on what was going on. Other groups were discussing what should be done in the days ahead.

Moshe was right. Don and I were the only people currently alive on earth at the gathering. But nearly every other person or being from heaven we had interacted with in the book was present: Melchizedek, Metatron, Enoch, Life, Abundance, Yeshua, Paul, David, Wisdom, Time, Holiness, Righteousness, and, of course, the three kings were there. I even noticed Immortality and Visions.

For hours, the conversation and activity in the room didn't diminish. I felt like we were at a New Year's Eve party. But instead of counting down to midnight, we anticipated something shifting with the 13th Mountain.

VISIONS

I spoke to as many guests as possible, thanking them for contributing to the book. But there was one guest I especially sought out. I had felt her presence the entire book. But she hadn't appeared—until now. As I approached a female figure with long hair wearing a gorgeous floor-length purple dress, I was struck by her stunning appearance.

"Visions," I called. "I'm so glad to connect before the book ends."

"The pleasure is all mine, Katharine," she answered.

"So many of us would love to have better visions. I know you open spiritual senses. You help us connect to heaven the way we were designed to. Could you do that for everyone who's reading the book?"

"Certainly," she smiled. "I happened to bring just the thing." From a hidden pocket in her dress, she pulled out a vial. "Put this on your eyes so you can see," Visions directed. "Sight for the blind. It's coming. Some people who have never seen before will see beyond their wildest dreams. Tell your story as a confirmation of my words."

As she spoke, I remembered telling people, "I can hear in the spiritual world, but I can't see. I'm not a seer." Then Yahweh told me he was going to give me a vision. I was thrilled. I thought I'd have one vision. I waited for a long time—for years. And nothing happened. But, slowly, my spiritual eyes opened. Now, I see visions all the time. I was standing in the King of Salem's house, surrounded by an all-star cast of heavenly figures, which was proof enough.

"Your journey parallels what all of humanity will go through. People will move from not seeing—or barely seeing—to being able to flow in visions in ways that will eventually change the whole universe," Visions told me in a firm voice. "Don't ask when. Ask how. Your journey is also the way it will open for the earth."

"I mostly practiced," I recalled. "I used worship to step into the heavenly realms. After a year of stepping into heaven daily through worship, I started seeing angels. After another year, I started seeing the cloud of witnesses. I spent time every day practicing as much as I could. Someone from heaven told me once that I ought to practice talking to people in heaven for thirty minutes a day. I thought that was ridiculous. No way did I have that much time. But I soon realized I spent far more time than that every day practicing."

"There's more," Visions prompted, nudging my memory as she spoke.

"I also did whatever I could to put myself in an environment that made it easier to connect with heaven. I worshiped. I met with others in ascension groups—groups that practiced going to heaven in a vision together. Those sorts of things helped open my senses. I'd take advantage of the atmosphere those things created to have as many encounters as I could. Eventually, I didn't need those things. But they helped initially."

"That's wonderful, Katharine. That's what I wanted you to share," Visions smiled.

"Do you have anything else to give us?" I asked hopefully.

After looking at me thoughtfully, she said, "Get Don and come back. There's something I want to say to both of you."

Nodding, I surveyed the room until I located Don. He was in an animated conversation with Holiness, Righteousness, and Immortality. As I approached them, I was tempted to eavesdrop on their discussion for a few minutes. I was sure it would be enlightening. But I didn't want to keep Visions waiting.

Once I explained, Don readily followed me to chat with Visions. As soon as we stood before her, she told Don, "You will restore the original blueprint for how humanity is supposed to receive communication from the spiritual realms. I've been commissioned to work with you."

Visions had spoken to me like one friend would speak to another. To Don, however, she spoke like you'd address a superior. I detected a reverent fear of him in her voice.

"So part of the blueprints in the Mountain is for heavenly

communication?" I asked.

"Certainly," Visions replied, "or I wouldn't be in this book. And Katharine, you can be a catalyst to what Don will do with that blueprint. You'll be like the yeast in a loaf of bread, making it rise and expand. In your own life, you can have heavenly communication flow as Yahweh designed it to. You'll also be able to do the same for other individuals. Don will do that for the entire earth."

"If you'll excuse us, I'd like to talk to Visions privately for a second," Don interjected.

"Of course," I replied. When Don pulled her off to the side, I did my best not to eavesdrop.

When they stepped back, Visions reached up to her head, where a translucent crown appeared. From the crown, she pulled off a single jewel. As soon as she did, an identical jewel grew in its place. She placed the jewel she had just removed from her crown in my hand and she said, "I'm giving you some of my authority over opening visions and spiritual senses in people. I'm doing so at his request," Visions' eyes veered in Don's direction. "Put the jewel in your crown. You'll use this authority to impart something to every reader of this book—and every future project of yours."

"Thank you," I replied, but part of me felt slightly insulted. It seemed like she was giving me something I already possessed. Couldn't she see that the most common feedback I received about my books *People from Heaven* and *Working with Angels*, for example, is that reading those books opened spiritual encounters for people—often for the first time? Then I realized that although most of me understood that being created in Yahweh's image meant I had far more authority than Visions herself, parts of my soul didn't remember who I am. Kindly, Visions was meeting those parts where they were, giving them something to hold onto—a jewel, an encounter with her, a promise—that would help those parts of my soul remember my divine nature. "I really do thank you," I told her again, this time including Don in my gratitude, too.

Smiling, Visions bowed slightly and took her leave.

To my surprise, the next time I saw Visions (outside of this book), I got hit with powerful authority over spiritual communication. My body shaking, I saw that the depth of the blueprint for visions—and the power and authority it carries—was far more potent than I realized. I was tempted to step back into the party and thank Visions and Don again. From many perspectives, what they opened to me was a treasure.

PATIO

"Have you seen the view from the patio?" Don asked as Visions retreated. "If not, you really should."

When I expressed interest, he motioned with his hand to head in that direction. As we wove through the crowd, he said, "There are some blueprints I've been meaning to tell you about. Before you leave, stop by, and I'll show them to you. If you're interested, come to a meeting we're having to discuss them. Salem invited a few of us to stay a couple extra days to begin working on the project. You should stay and work with us."

When he finished talking, we had reached the balcony on the rooftop patio. A railing bordered the entire patio. But Salem had used glass rather than stone for the railing. In daylight hours, you could sit in any spot and have an unobstructed view of the landscape. At night, however, what lay below us was shrouded in darkness. The most captivating view was spread above our heads. The stars felt even more majestic at this height.

As a cool breeze swept past us, I said, "You've just answered my last question for this book—What's next? Sure, I'll take a look at the plans you brought."

"What's next, Katharine, is we build. Now that the mountain is open and we've celebrated that opening, the real work begins. We get to build this stuff."

"I've known that I'm meant to build the original design for heaven and earth for far longer than I've known you. But meeting you and the people and beings here—many that you've introduced me to or taken my relationship with them deeper—my understanding of what it means to build original design has gone so much deeper. I feel like I'm better positioned to do it. I hope this book does the same thing for people.

"Those drawn to this book, Don, will also be meant to build the new heaven and new earth. Some of them will have known that for years. For others, that awareness will begin to reach their consciousness. I hope that by meeting the people and beings here—and connecting with those of us on earth—we'll all be able to do things faster and better."

Don nodded in agreement.

NEXT STEPS

At that moment, Yahweh appeared. I didn't see his form. But I could feel his presence hovering near us. He was actually hovering on the other side of the railing—several stories off the ground.

"You wonder what's next," Yahweh began. "Both of you, stretch out your arms."

Like earlier in the book, we both extended our arms. This time, however, it looked like we were reaching into the cosmos themselves.

"Your reach will go far," Yahweh told us. "Your impact will extend over all the earth and into the heavens. Begin to extend your reach now."

Then I understood. Earlier, by the brook, we had extended our arms over the earth. Now, we were extending our arms over the heavens. Symbolically, Yahweh showed us that our reach—our influence and capacity to shift things—was over both places. Both times he asked us to extend our arms, his words felt weighty. This time, with the cosmos in the backdrop, they also felt majestic.

When we rested our arms at our sides again, Yahweh continued. "I've hidden some of the blueprints for the new heaven and new earth in heaven's mysteries. The mysteries you've both held inside you have contained some of those blueprints. So you are already well acquainted with certain blueprints. But now, all the blueprints have been placed in the Mountain. There is so much there that it would take most people a lifetime to just sort through them. I don't want it to take a lifetime. So I'm releasing to you an understanding of what is housed in that Mountain."

As he spoke, Yahweh was also breathing on us. In his last breath, he took us inside the Mountain, releasing a map of its contents into our spirits. Visually, it looked to me like a map you may download when visiting an amusement park and want to know where to go in what order. So, the map Yahweh downloaded contained the location of everything and an understanding of it so we could decide the best order to tackle things.

Yahweh turned to me, "Every part of the Mountain needs to be combed through. Each section needs to be distributed to the right people. Then, the tools and technology to help people build their part must be sorted through and given to the people who will do the most with it. Katharine, I'm placing you on the Distribution Committee." As he spoke, Yahweh downloaded specific instructions about my role on the committee.

Turning to Don, he said, "You will be a Father in this Tribe. With your leadership, exponentially more will be accomplished than could be without you. Every generation coming from your loins will also walk in the highest levels of leadership. I am establishing your house as a dynasty. Like how I made my servant David's house into a dynasty to stand before me forever, I do the same with your name."

THANK-YOU GIFT

I was smiling from ear to ear at what Yahweh was speaking over Don when Yahweh said, "Katharine, I'd like to give you a thank-you gift for writing this book for me." Moving inches from my face, he breathed, "I'm giving you a never-ending life. You may live on earth for as long as you want."

"Wow, thank you," I replied, stunned. "But isn't that a bit much for simply writing a book?"

"This wasn't an ordinary book for you," Yahweh replied. "To publish this book, you had to lay down what was most important to you spiritually. Several years ago, I asked you to open a mystery with me on earth. I warned you that if you said yes, it would cost you everything. Then I watched you give up everything precious to you for that mystery because you knew how much it would mean to me to have it opened. That moved me. But you learned that dying *for* a mystery or spiritual truth is only half of what's needed, didn't you? Go on, explain what else I required of you."

"You asked me to be willing to die *to* the mystery, not just *for* it," I replied, my eyes unable to meet his. "We think we're being super spiritual when we're willing to sacrifice everything for a truth to be opened on earth. That's not wrong. It's just not all of what's needed to administer a mystery well."

"We have to live in constant, full surrender to what is best for others and not what is best for ourselves," Don explained.

"Otherwise, we end up sacrificing everything for a limited understanding of the truth and not for Truth itself," I added, looking at Yahweh. He was Truth. He's what mattered. "We have to die to revelations and insights we've had—to be willing to walk away from them if you whisper that there's something greater. If we don't, we stay stuck in the partial revelations of the past. We're unable to move into the fullness of who you are."

"So tell people what I asked you to do," Yahweh prodded.

"You asked me to take the most precious thing I had with you and lay it at *his* feet," I blurted in an animated voice as I glanced at Don. "I thought it was ridiculous at first."

"No, you didn't. You knew it was wisdom," Yahweh reminded calmly.

"Okay, maybe I did. But I didn't want to," I admitted.

"But it was the best thing to do," Don chimed in.

"So what happened?" Yahweh nudged.

A thousand emotions rose to my throat, competing to express my answer to him. "I . . . He . . ." I faltered.

"You acted wisely, Katharine. That's what happened," Yahweh answered his own question. "You laid down what you thought was everything. That moved my heart deeply. And when Don told you what you possessed was only a partial understanding of me and my ways, you didn't argue. You swallowed your pride to embrace a fuller understanding of me. You were willing to leave behind a partial understanding of truth to go after my heart. And you were willing to do that without regard for yourself. You were thinking of others.

"You criticize yourself for how you didn't handle everything perfectly. But I wasn't looking for perfect execution. I was looking at your heart— at what you were willing to sacrifice for me. And I was looking at how you would administer anything I entrusted to you. Do you know what I concluded?"

"That you need to give me an unbelievable amount of time to transition?" I joked. The whole process had taken a lot longer than I thought it would.

"Perhaps," he chuckled. "My conclusion was you administered what I entrusted to you by putting the interests of others—on earth and in heaven—above your own interests. You proved ready to administer far more than I originally entrusted you with. I'm giving you the right to administer not just one mystery but every mystery."

He stepped back to emphasize his next words. "I give you the staff, office space, understanding, and authority to administer every mystery in creation." As he spoke, I felt things rising inside me to take on that role. I also knew his words were an invitation to others—and a promise that he would give them the same things he was giving me if they made the same kind of decisions I had.

Hovering inches from my face again, Yahweh told me, "What you've experienced with me so far has been a taste, Katharine. Because you were willing to lay down your taste—the partial understanding that seemed like everything to you—I open the entire banquet to you. You will be one of the first people to experience the fullness of who I am."

I was too stunned to respond.

Yahweh's presence didn't leave. But my awareness of him slowly faded. Gradually, I became more conscious of what Don was thinking than what Yahweh was contemplating. Don was excited for me—and filled with holy awe at the weight of all Yahweh's words. We both stood silently, unable to speak, as what Yahweh had told us sank in.

Before we could fully process things, though, Salem called everyone inside. He had an announcement to make.

RARE WINE

After gathering the whole room's attention, Salem said, "Thank you for making this event—and this book—possible. My house, as well as my heart, thank you in the deepest ways. I hope these events will open a rich, working flow among us for one purpose—building the new heaven and new earth in the greatest way possible."

Light applause broke out in the crowd. A few people cheered.

"And now, I have a special treat," the king continued. "To facilitate our working relationship, I'm pouring wine from my private vintage."

Proudly, Salem held up a bottle of his rare wine. Real gold encased the cork on the elegantly hand-crafted bottle. When Salem released the cork, wine shot upwards and rained down on many of us at the gathering. I couldn't tell if he had meant to soak his guests so thoroughly or if he had grabbed a sparkling wine by mistake.

"Or rather, I'm baptizing you all with my wine tonight," Salem laughed.

"That may be the best way to taste a wine, Salem," someone shouted.

BEST FOR LAST

Staff circulated with glasses of the wine on small trays. I helped myself to one and took a seat near the center of the row of sofas and chairs lining the sliding glass doors. Before long, Moshe and Don wandered over and sat on either side of me. Salem himself joined us moments later, settling next to Don.

The four of us talked, laughed, and strategized as we absorbed the breathtaking views from the highest point in Salem's house. Many people and beings contributed to this book. The room was full of them. Below us, the entire house was filled with other distinguished guests whose presence had impacted our last few days together. But the three men surrounding me had contributed uniquely to this book. They carried authority over it. It felt like they were a bench of three judges—guiding the book to have its greatest impact.

"This is a good way to end the book," Don remarked as morning drew near. "We're surrounded by the people and beings who filled the pages of this book. The view of what we need to do going forward couldn't be more breathtaking from this spot. Look around you, Katharine. Few books have a picturesque moment like this unfold right at their climax."

"He's right," Moshe chimed in. "What could make a better ending than sitting on the rooftop of the person administering the blueprints for the new heaven and new earth—"

"As the sun rises on the third day since the events here began," Don added.

"I don't think there could be a better way to end this book," Salem agreed.

"I guess you're right," I decided as the first rays of light peeked over the horizon, filling the landscape with brilliant hope. "Is that the 13th Mountain in the distance—the place where the blueprints are kept?"

"It is," Salem nodded.

We watched in silence as the sun slowly illuminated the mountain.

"This is a moment to be treasured," Moshe told us. "Never to be forgotten."

"Not in all the years of our immortality?" I grinned.

"Not for at least a million years," Don answered, smiling. "Everything the earth has ever wanted is about to become a reality."

ABOUT THE AUTHORS

Katharine Wang is a co-founder of Age to Come University (www. ATCUniversity.com).  She's earned a Masters in Theological Studies from Liberty Baptist Theological Seminary and a J.D. from Yale Law School. After litigating high-profile lawsuits in Washington, D.C., Katharine's focused on unlocking people's deepest potentials. She's founded a non-profit, created a free app for kids (Kingdom Keys Bible App), hosted a radio show, and coached people in nearly every continent. Her books and courses have transformed lives around the world. She enjoys good books, fun family hikes, and stimulating conversations.

As a fervent and thoughtful trailblazer, Don Joseph is on a journey to  uncover the depths of Yahweh's heart. He began his career facilitating transactions for high networth individuals in Australia's banking sector. Don's passion for understanding has unlocked mysteries spanning from wealth and finance to the intricacies of the human soul. He is a coach, mentor, and friend to many worldwide. Alongside his spiritual pursuits, he delights in sports, cinema, and meaningful connections and dialogue.

Also by Katharine Wang

People from Heaven
Living Loved
Faces of God
Working with Angels

Become an Insider!

Insiders receive:

↜ Exclusive messages from Katharine & Don

↜ Free bonus content

↜ Connection with others

↜ Sneak peaks at the next books

Sign up for free on the website:

www.ATCUniversity.com/chronicles

Made in the USA
Columbia, SC
26 December 2024

50644222R00117